tim bowler

PLAYING DEAD

Blade is hiding.

Playing dead.

He knows people are looking for him, but he doesn't want to be found. Because he knows these people aren't messing about.

But Blade can look after himself.

He has to . . .

From the Carnegie Medal-winning author of *River Boy*, *Starseeker*, and *Frozen Fire* comes something completely different — the first title in a startlingly compelling new series. Contemporary, pacy, and utterly gripping, *Blade* takes you on a roller-coaster ride through the secret, dangerous life of its unforgettable narrator.

Other Books by Tim Bowler

Blade: Closing In

Midget
Dragon's Rock
River Boy
Shadows
Storm Catchers
Starseeker
Apocalypse
Frozen Fire

tim bowler

winner of the carnegie medal

BLADE

PLAYING DEAD

book 1

OXFORD
UNIVERSITY PRESS

OXFORD
UNIVERSITY PRESS

Great Clarendon Street, Oxford OX2 6DP

Oxford University Press is a department of the University of Oxford.
It furthers the University's objective of excellence in research, scholarship,
and education by publishing worldwide in

Oxford   New York

Auckland   Cape Town   Dar es Salaam   Hong Kong   Karachi
Kuala Lumpur   Madrid   Melbourne   Mexico City   Nairobi
New Delhi   Shanghai   Taipei   Toronto

With offices in

Argentina   Austria   Brazil   Chile   Czech Republic   France   Greece
Guatemala   Hungary   Italy   Japan   Poland   Portugal   Singapore
South Korea   Switzerland   Thailand   Turkey   Ukraine   Vietnam

Oxford is a registered trade mark of Oxford University Press
in the UK and in certain other countries

British Library Cataloguing in Publication Data

Data available

ISBN: 978-0-19-275484-4

3 5 7 9 10 8 6 4 2

Typeset in Meridien by TnQ Books and Journals Pvt. Ltd.,
Chennai, India

Printed in Great Britain by Cox and Wyman Ltd, Reading, Berkshire

Paper used in the production of this book is a natural, recyclable product made
from wood grown in sustainable forests. The manufacturing process conforms
to the environmental regulations of the country of origin.

For Rachel
with my love

So he's looking at me with his puggy face, this big jerk of a policeman, and I'm thinking, take him out or let him live?

Big question.

I don't like questions. Questions are about choices and choices are a pain. I like certainties. Got to do this, got to do that, no debate. Take him out, let him live. Know what you got to do. Certainty.

Only I'm not certain here. I'm pretty sure I want to take him out. I hate the sight of him and I hate being back at the police station.

The knife feels good hidden inside my sock. Pugface didn't even feel it when he frisked me. But he'll feel it pretty quick if he doesn't treat me right. It's only a small blade but I know how to use it.

He's still watching me with those pig-eyes.

'Right, young man,' he says.

'I'm not your young man.'

He takes no notice. He's too busy smirking.

'In your own words,' he goes on.

'In your own words what?'

'In your own words—what happened?'

'What happened where?'

He gives this heavy, exaggerated sigh. I hate that. Move my fingers slowly down my thigh.

He can't see with the desk in the way. That bosomy policewoman over by the door's watching but she can't see anything either. I can tell from her face.

Anyway, she's too far away. I can have my knife out and into Pugface before she's covered half the ground between us. Probably time to stick her too.

He goes on in that patronizing voice.

'What happened at the pedestrian crossing?'

My fingers are close to the knife now. I stop my

hand. No need to move it any further. I'm safe enough. All that's needed is a lunge and a thrust. Maybe a bit more if Bosoms gets involved.

'What happened at the crossing?' says Pugface.

'Nothing.'

'You stood in the road after the lights had turned to green and refused to move and let the traffic pass.'

'Did I?'

'You shouted abuse at the drivers waiting to move on.'

'Can't remember.'

'Especially the man in the nearest car.'

'Can't remember.'

'The man in the green estate. He asked you to move aside so that he and everybody else could drive on. You swore back at him and made obscene gestures.'

'He was rude to me.'

'You don't think maybe you were the one being rude?'

I shrug. I'm starting to enjoy this now.

'Eh?' says Pugface.

'Don't know.'

'It was dangerous.'

'No, it wasn't. He was never going to run me over.'

'Because unlike you, he had some sense of responsibility. Though it would have shaken you up quite a bit if he had put his foot down and driven at you. I don't doubt you'd have moved aside pretty quickly if he'd done that.'

'He wouldn't have had the guts.'

'Is that what you think stopped him? Lack of guts?'

'Yeah.'

'That's what you'd have done, is it? If you'd been the driver and you'd seen some rude little kid standing on the crossing and refusing to move? Jeering and swearing at you, and daring you to drive on? You'd have put your foot down and run him over, would you?'

'Too right.'

He leans back in the chair, glances at Bosoms. I'm really having fun now. They're both out of their depth. They don't know what to do with me. They know they can't prosecute or anything. It's just not that big a deal. I'll get a warning, nothing more.

Then Pugface stands up.

'Seems like we've got a problem, then.'

He moves round the desk towards me. I don't like the look of him suddenly. Don't know why. He sits on the edge of the desk.

Too close. Don't like people that close. Makes me remember things. I think of the knife, squeeze my hands into a ball. He glances at Bosoms again, then back at me.

'The driver's told us he doesn't wish to take things further. He just wanted to report the incident.'

Say nothing.

'He was a bit worried we might not be able to trace the boy who held up the traffic for five minutes, swore at all the drivers, then ran off.' Pugface sniffs. 'He clearly wasn't aware just how well we know you round here.'

He leans closer. I'm hating this now. It's not the police station. It's this face leering down at me. He's got to pull back. He's got to do it now, right now.

But he doesn't. He just smirks again—then leans even closer.

'Do you really think,' he whispers, 'that we haven't

noticed you've got something hidden inside your sock?'

I lunge for the knife—in vain. The man's hands are tight round my arms. I don't even see the woman move. One minute she's over by the door, the next she's behind me, pulling me back against the chair. I spit at 'em, snarl at 'em, try to break free. Doesn't do any good.

'Bastards!' I'm rocking about, screaming my head off. 'Bloody bastards!'

'Yeah, yeah,' says Pugface. 'Bloody bastards.'

'Got a nice tongue on him,' says the woman.

'Bastards!' I scream.

'Look inside his sock,' mutters the policeman.

The woman pulls out the knife, fumbles with the other sock.

'There's nothing in there,' I yell.

She checks anyway, then straightens up, holding the knife. The man lets go of me and takes it from her. I duck under their arms and make a dash for the door.

I'm not fast—no point pretending—but being small sometimes helps, and somehow I've taken 'em by surprise. I'm at the door before 'em. I can see Pugface's hands clutching at me, and the woman's, but they're kind of falling over each other.

Then I'm out in the corridor.

Shouts from inside the room. Some constable running towards me from the desk. That's when fire extinguishers come in handy. A squirt over the guy and he slips. Jump over him and out the door.

Nothing to it.

And that was when I was seven.

Now that I've turned fourteen, I look back and you know what's weird? It's like nothing's changed. I still don't like the police and I still don't like people getting close.

And that includes you, Bigeyes.

Not quite sure why I'm talking to you at all. I don't even know you. Maybe it's something Becky said to me. You got to make sense of your life. You got to think about what you're doing. You got to think before you act. And if you ever want to talk, I'm here for you.

Except Becky's dead.

So maybe that's why I'm dumping on you.

Not that I feel obliged to tell you the truth, mind. Don't get any ideas. I mean, I might tell you the truth but I might not. Just so you know.

I call the shots here. I choose what I say and what I don't. You can choose whether to stay or wig it somewhere else. And if you choose to wig it, that's fine with me. I don't need you. Remember that.

I don't need anyone.

Thing about lying—we're all told it's wrong. Tell the truth, tell the truth, tell the truth. But where's that ever got anyone? I've been lying since as long as I can remember. Why? Cos everyone I've ever known has lied to me.

So what am I going to tell you? Not much, so don't get excited. You probably want to know my name. Well, that's a bit of a problem. I got loads.

There's the name I was given as a baby but that's a dronky name so I never use it. Then there's the names I make up. I got binbags of those. Different names for different people. Depends on where I am and who I'm with.

But there is one name I like.

It's the name Becky gave me. A name from the past. Everybody called me it in the old days. No one does now cos no one in this city knows it. And that's fine. I don't like to remember. But I do like the name. You can use it if you want.

BLADE.

That's what they used to call me. And I liked it. Bit of style, bit of clash. But remember—it's a secret. Don't be a claphead and spew it. If I find out you've blotched on me, then you'll find out why Becky called me Blade.

As for the rest of the world, I don't give two bells what people call me. Why fuss about a name when you can make 'em up so easy? And you know what? Life's a bit like that too.

Easy, simple, no sweat.

What you shaking your head for? Don't believe me? Well, I don't care. Believe what you like. It's true anyway. Life's a whack. It's no big deal coping with stuff. Other people—they make a horse trough out of it, get stressed out. Me, I'm different.

It's like I'm on top of this mountain, this great big mountain, higher than all the others, higher than—what's it called?—Everest. Miles higher. I'm all on my own with my head way up above everybody else, and I'm fine about it. There's no one'll ever conquer me, cos no one'll ever get near me.

You listening to this, Bigeyes?

That's what it's about. It's about seeing things from a higher place than everybody else. Seeing things no one else can.

Like that guy in Café Blue Sox. I can see things about him no one else can. I can see things about him even he can't see. Got him? Table by the window. Not the guy with the vomity hair. He'll be leaving in a minute. Don't ask me how I know.

The other guy, the one with the mobile phone. Brown hair, about twenty, bit smooth. Got him?

There's loads like him round here. Big head, small brain. This city breeds 'em. Very easy meat. He'll finish his phone call in a minute, drape his coat over the back of that empty chair next to him, and forget about it.

Why? Cos all his attention'll be taken up with that blonde girl behind the bar.

There you go. What did I tell you? Vomity's leaving.

Now—watch Dogbrain. There he goes, see? Mobile down, sip of coffee, coat over the chair.

Walk over, stand outside, wander in. Busy place, lots of yak. Even better.

No one notices me. I'm good at that. No one notices me when I don't want 'em to. I might be invisible. Only the red-lipped girl behind the bar sees me, and that's just cos I want a coffee.

Blondie's already over by the window talking to Dogbrain.

'Can I help you?' says Redlips.

'Latte, please. Medium.'

She fixes me the latte. Take it over to the window. Blondie's still there, leaning over the guy's chair. They're talking about nothing. Murmurs, giggles.

Sit down at the next table. They don't notice. Move the chair closer to his. More murmurs, giggles. They're talking about a guy he knows, some dungpot called Kenny.

Check round me, check the guy, check the girl.

Nobody even knows I'm here. I might be a dream, a spirit. I love doing this. I know where the wallet is. I can see the shape of it from here. Inside pocket of the jacket, closed with a zip.

Another check round—stop. Blondie's straightened up. She's looking me over. But she's not noticing me. She's thinking of Dogbrain even as she looks at me.

The guy hasn't even turned. He's drinking her up with his eyes like she's some kind of cocktail. She looks back at him, leans down again, puts a hand on his shoulder.

Two minutes later I've drunk my latte and gone. And I've got a nice fat wallet.

I've also got a problem.

I'm being followed.

Can't see anyone but someone's after me. Don't ask me how I know.

Keep a lookout, Bigeyes.

It's not Dogbrain. I know that much. It's no one from Café Blue Sox. It's someone else. More than one person too. I can feel eyes on me from several places. Don't distract me. I need to work out how many people there are.

Four at least. Maybe more. Hard to tell.

Look behind. Check the High Street.

Nobody. Nobody dangerous anyway. Lots of people but they're all muffins.

Walk on.

Two men, big hairy gobbos like they're off a building site. It's not them. Another gobbo coming the other way. But he's running for a bus.

Danger's still there. I can feel it. Which way? Left or right? Never mind, I'll decide. Left, down to the end of Crowstone Road, right at the bottom, down the pedestrian precinct.

Walk, walk, walk.

Still don't feel right. There's definitely more than four people. I can feel at least five, maybe more.

Glance round.

Nobody.

Walk on. End of the precinct, down the alleyway, hurry through it to Meadway Drive, on towards the canal. Don't run. They'll think I'm scared. Just keep walking, fast. Still a few people around but they're thinning out.

The canal looks quiet and the towpath's deserted.

Not a good place to go but I can maybe cut across one of the bridges further down and shake 'em off round the industrial estate.

It's a mistake. I know it the moment I set off down the towpath. Three figures in front of me. Trixi and two mates. If they've been following, they must have raced ahead and climbed over the fence. So where are the rest?

Look behind.

Three more covering my escape.

Shit, this is bad. Don't let anyone tell you girl gangs are a softer touch than boy gangs. They're worse. They fight dirty. And here's me with no weapon.

Trixi gives me a mocking little call.

'Hey, Slicky!'

They move in. I look about me. Canal on the left, fence on the right. Nothing for it. I make a dash for the fence.

But they catch me easy.

You can't fight six of 'em. I wouldn't want to take on one of 'em. Not these trolls. Boy gangs are another thing. There's always one or two muffins in there you can have a go at. Not this lot. You don't even get in the gang unless you've proved yourself and done some serious damage.

'Pull him back!' says Trixi.

They pull me back, throw me down on the towpath.

'Silly boy,' she says, looking down.

'Trix. Lay off me.'

'What you got?'

'Nothing.'

I look up at the faces. Flint-eyes, flint-hearts. I don't even want to know what they're carrying.

'I got nothing, Trix.'

'Stupid kid.'

Say nothing. Let her call me a kid. She's older anyway. They're all about sixteen. She can call me a kid.

'Stupid kid,' she says again.

'I got nothing, Trix.'

'No wallet?'

'No.'

She kicks me hard in the ribs.

'Ow!'

'No wallet?' she says.

It's stupid holding out. They're going to take everything anyway.

'Listen, Trix, I—'

'Check his pockets,' she says.

They poke about, pull everything out.

'What a surprise,' says Trixi. She holds up Dogbrain's wallet. 'What else has he got?'

'Another wallet,' says Sash.

'And another,' says Tammy.

'Busy boy, aren't we?' says Trixi.

'Trix, listen—'

'Sort him,' she says flatly.

They sort me, five of 'em. Trix doesn't get involved. I'm glad of that. She's the worst. But it's still bad. They beat the shit out of me, then stand back, breathing hard. I lie there on the towpath, aching for 'em to go. I can feel the scratches on my face, the blood in my mouth, the bruises all over my body.

Trixi steps forward and looks down.

'Just one last thing,' she says.

I brace myself. She's going to kick me in the head. I know it. But I'm wrong.

'Finish it,' she says to the girls.

And they crowd round again. I close into a ball. I've got no idea what 'finish it' means but it's going to be bad. They yank my arms back. I wrestle free and close up again. Trixi kicks me in the back.

'Ah!'

'You'll make it worse,' she says and then, 'Finish it,' to the girls.

They force my arms back again, and now I know what they're doing.

'Don't!' I shout. 'Please!'

But I can't stop 'em. My clothes are coming off. The jacket first, then the jumper and shirt, then the shoes, socks, trousers. Only the pants left.

'No.' I'm looking up at them. 'Please.'

They don't even hear me. Off come the pants, and I'm lying there naked. They stand back and I close up into a ball again. I want to cry. Christ, I want to cry so much.

Don't bloody cry.

They're still standing round me, still looking down.

'Trix, listen—'

'Shut up.'

'Trix!'

'I said shut up.' She looks down at me with contempt. Enjoyment too. There's no missing that. I'm hugging my knees to my chest, shivering, shaking, fighting tears.

Don't cry. Don't bloody cry.

'Can't see you very well,' she says in a low voice.

I say nothing. I don't dare to speak. Trixi glances at her mates, then simply nods. They lean down again.

'No!' I shout.

They force my arms back again, stretch me out, spine against the ground.

Don't cry. Don't bloody cry.

Trixi's looking me over down below.

'Oh, dear,' she says. 'How disappointing.'

Don't cry. Please.

I'm begging myself now. Begging myself not to cry.

She pulls out a knife, flicks it open.

'Don't!' I'm screaming at her. 'Don't!'

She laughs. The girls start laughing too. She leans down, plays with the knife.

'Don't what?' she says quietly.

Now the tears come. They flood my eyes so deeply Trixi's face becomes a blur. All I see is the glint of the blade. I feel the scratches on my face sting as the tears run over them.

'Don't,' I murmur. 'Please don't.'

I'm weeping now, weeping like a kid who wants his mummy. Somehow my eyes clear. I see Trixi lean closer. I see the blade approach my face, then move slowly down my body, an inch from the skin.

More tears flood my eyes. I lose sight of her again, then feel my arms and legs released, hear the sound of laughter, and the ripping of fabric. I wipe my eyes with the back of my hand and stare.

The knife's at work but not on me. She's cutting up my clothes. I don't speak, don't move. There's no point. The girls'll do what they want. They've all got knives out now and they're slashing the trousers, shirt, jacket, everything, even the pants.

They throw the shoes into the canal and chuck the shredded remains of my clothes in after them. Trixi looks down at me and smiles.

'See you around,' she says.

And they're gone.

Yeah, all right. I know what you're thinking. You're thinking the first lie was when I said I find life easy and the second was when I said I don't need anyone.

But I already admitted I tell lies. You can't pretend I didn't. So there's no point looking at me like that.

Shit, I'm freezing.

Got to find some clothes, got to find somewhere warm. But clothes first. Stand up. Come on. Do it. Christ, I'm swaying on my feet.

Don't just stare at me, Bigeyes. See if you can rescue some of my clothes. No, forget that. They're ruined. Do something else. I don't know. See if you can find something I can wrap round me. A blanket or an old newspaper, whatever.

I know it's a long shot. There's nothing much round here. Just the canal, towpath, bushes, fence.

Walk. Best to walk. Don't go back to the city centre. Head for the industrial estate. Someone there might have a spare coat or something.

Walk, walk, walk.

I'm aching all over. Those trolls know how to hurt. And I'm crying again. Wish I could stop but I can't. See that? You were thinking I was just a cocky little tick. Well, I am a cocky little tick but I got feelings too.

Who the hell are those people on the towpath?

Women joggers in matching tracksuits. Three of 'em, talking as they run. Just what I need. Still, at least they won't be scared of me like this. Give 'em a shout.

'Hoy!'

They've seen me.

'Hoy!'

I don't believe it. They're turning back.

'Hoy! Stop!'

They're not stopping. They're putting on speed.

'Hoy! I need help!'

They've gone. Didn't look back once.

Walk on. Shiver, shiver, shiver. God, I hate November. Cold, grey, depressing. Getting dark already. Not a soul in sight since the women ran off.

Hang on. I'm wrong.

Another woman on the towpath but she's no jogger. She's old. White hair, shuffly walk. She shouldn't be out here on her own. Wait a minute. There's something moving in the bushes, something black.

A rottweiler. Whitehair's not so dumb after all. She's spotted me. She's coming on.

Walk. Act confident. No point covering your dingers. She's already seen 'em.

Dog's out of the bushes now, running towards me. She calls out.

'Buffy!'

Dog stops at the sound of her voice. Whitehair comes on. Doesn't look nervous like those joggers did. Stops by the dog, bends down, fits a leash to the collar. I've stopped too. I'm keeping well back from that rottweiler.

Whitehair looks up at me.

'What's happened?' she says.

Sounds Irish. I don't answer. Don't know why. Can't speak.

'You've got blood all round your face,' she says. 'And scratches everywhere. What's happened to you?'

'Got beaten up.'

The woman shakes her head.

'You poor thing.'

She starts to take off her coat.

'No,' I begin.

But I say no more. I'm dying to wear the coat. I don't care what it looks like. I just want to be warm.

I just want to be covered up.

'Put this on,' she says.

She walks towards me, holding the coat in one hand and the dog's lead in the other.

'Don't worry about Buffy,' she says. 'She looks fearsome and if you attacked me, she'd turn nasty. But once she's decided you're a friend, you've got nothing to fear. And she's clearly decided that already.'

So it seems. The dog's rubbing herself against me like we're old mates.

I put on the woman's coat.

'Now you're going to get cold,' I say.

'Don't worry about me,' she says. 'Let's get you sorted out. Come on.'

She turns and starts to lead me back the way she's come along the towpath.

'Where we going?' I say.

'To my house. It's just over the first bridge. Not very luxurious, I'm afraid, but it's warm and we can ring the police from there.'

'No!'

I stop.

She looks round at me.

'Are you in trouble with the police?'

'No, but I don't like 'em.'

The woman shrugs.

'Well, we'll talk about what to do later. Let's just get to the house.'

We walk on in silence.

And you know what, Bigeyes? I'm getting scared again. Don't know why. I'm not scared of this woman. She's nice. Must be seventy, at least, maybe older. Not too steady on her legs.

But I'm scared, really scared. Like something's about to happen only I don't know what. Might sound crazy but I trust my feelings so I'm looking about me as cute as I can.

Trouble is, I'm so cold I can't think. Coat's nice and thick and I've got all the buttons done up, but the air's getting in everywhere. The ground's hard on my bare feet. I'm still stinging all over. My nostrils feel crusted up. Dried blood probably.

I must look a mess.

Whitehair's cold too. She's got one of those scruffy cardigans on with buttons up the front and a scraggy old dress down to her shoes, but she's shivering.

'I'm sorry,' I say.

'What for, dear?'

'Making you shiver.'

She gives me a smile.

'You're shivering far more than me and I'm not surprised. That coat will only take off the worst of the chill. But we'll soon have you warm at least. Two more minutes and we're there. See? Just beyond the bridge. That's my house.'

And there it is—a little bungalow all by itself on the other side of the canal.

And you know what's weird? I must have passed this place a thousand times and yet now, as I'm hobbling towards it with this white-haired old woman, it's like I've never seen it before.

And I'm still feeling scared.

She opens the door of the bungalow.

'In you go,' she says.

I don't want to go. Don't ask me why. I'm still freezing. The coat's not doing much to help. Here's a house and a friendly old woman, and she's offering me shelter. And I don't want to go in.

'Go on,' she says. 'You need to get warm.'

Still don't move.

She watches me. She's either confused or angry. Can't tell.

'I'll go in,' she says, 'and I'll leave the door open. You come on in if you want. But if you're not going to come in, can you leave the coat on the step? It's the only decent thing I've got for cold weather.'

And in she goes.

Buffy's already charged ahead. God knows where she's disappeared to but I can hear her thumping about in one of the rooms.

Whitehair's halfway down the hall, not even glancing back at me.

It looks a poky little place, not much furniture and pretty ropy stuff at that. Carpet's knackered too, frayed all over with gaps showing the floorboards underneath.

I'm still standing on the step feeling like a dimp. I just want Whitehair to turn round. I don't know why. But she's still heading down the hall to the end.

I walk in, close the door behind me. Don't feel

better. Warmer but not better. There's a musty smell in this place, like she never cleans it or never lives in it or something. Can't work out what it is.

And I'm getting flashbacks. I've been in a place like this before.

Don't bother asking me where cos I'm not telling you.

Buffy's running back down the hall with an old shoe in her mouth. I suppose this is a present.

'No, thanks.'

She drops it at my feet.

'No, thanks.'

I'm still feeling strange. I want to turn and run. I don't like these flashbacks.

Whitehair's disappeared into one of the rooms off the hall. I can hear noises like drawers being pulled open. Buffy shoves her head against my bare leg. I push her away. She does it again. She thinks I'm playing.

More flashbacks. I hate this place. I'm really scared. I'm shaking. I can't go outside, not without any clothes, and I can't stay. This place feels all wrong and here's Whitehair coming back. She's carrying a bundle of clothes.

'Now, then,' she says, 'I don't know if any of these'll fit. Buffy, get out of the way.'

She pushes open the door to the room on my left. I go in. A little bedroom. Spare, scrawny, funny smell, just like the rest of the house.

'You can use this room,' she says. 'Try on the clothes. They used to belong to my grandson.'

I'm not even going to tell her she's lying. What's the point? But she is. I got an instinct for lies. I can always tell when someone's zipping me over.

Don't ask me how I know.

But I'm not going to make a fuss. I need some clothes and these are clothes. Crap clothes and probably a bad fit but better than no clothes at all.

She dumps 'em in my arms and closes the door on me.

Turns out they're not bad. Bit baggy and definitely not my style but enough to get me away from here. A knock on the door, then Whitehair's voice.

'Are you decent?'

I open the door.

'How do they feel?' says Whitehair.

She's looking me over, Buffy next to her, thumping her tail on the floor.

'Jumper looks nice and thick,' she says. 'Bit long but better that than too short. I'll get you a belt and those trousers will feel better. We'll sort out some shoes for you later. Now then—we must ring your parents at once.'

And this silence falls between us.

Buffy picks it up and stops banging her tail against the floor. Whitehair's watching me closely. First time I've noticed she's got green eyes. They're not unfriendly but I've stopped trusting her.

'Why don't you trust me?' she says.

She's speaking my thoughts for me now. I don't answer. She gives me this smile. Don't trust that either.

'Is it because you don't trust anyone?' she says.

'What are you, a shrink?'

She doesn't answer that, just shrugs.

'Where do you live?' she says eventually. 'I can order a taxi to get you home. I'll pay for it.'

I'm not telling her anything. It's none of her business. And I'm not telling you anything either,

Bigeyes, so don't keep looking at me.

I'm getting more uneasy by the minute. Whitehair's too close.

'Move back.' I glare at her. 'Move back.'

She stays where she is, just watches.

'My name's Mary,' she says.

Her voice has changed. It's really low, like she doesn't want me to hear it, like I've got to stay this close to her if I'm going to hear it. I take a step back.

She doesn't move, just goes on watching, then speaks again, same low voice.

'I'm from Ireland. Small village down in the south.'

Like I give two bells where she comes from. She can come from the North Pole for all I care. She's not what she pretends to be. I know it.

'Do you want to tell me your name?' she says.

I can see her green eyes moving over me. What's she looking at? She should keep her eyes on my face.

'I'm watching your hands,' she says suddenly. 'I can see I'm making you nervous. But you're making me nervous now. So I'm watching your hands.'

'What for?'

'In case you attack me.'

'Keep your distance and I won't.'

Another big silence. We're both staring at each other. I glance at Buffy. She's watching me too, and she's changed. We're not friends now. She's picked up I might be trouble. She'll rip me apart if I go for Mary.

'What are you frightened of?' says the old woman.

'Not you.'

'What are you frightened of?'

I don't answer. I'm watching Buffy. She's all tensed up, like she's going to jump or snap.

'Buffy,' says Mary. 'Easy, easy.'

Her voice is like a murmur now. The dog relaxes. Mary's eyes look suddenly soft. Soft and green. She looks back at me.

'Come and have some tea,' she says.

The kitchen. Is this dronky or what? Look at that stove. Something from the Dark Ages. Not much in the way of lighting either. Mary's burning a candle, one of those fat, scented ones. She's got it on a saucer on the table.

'Sit down,' she says.

Buffy's close by. Looks confused. Doesn't know whether to lick my hand or bite it off.

I sit down at the table. Candle's flickering. Mary's lighting another one over on the shelf. She sits down, other side of the table. I can see she's keeping her distance.

Fine by me. She looks at me. I look back.

'Yeah?'

'Easy,' she says.

I feel Buffy's nose against my hand. Stroke her. She licks my palm. Mary smiles.

'She trusts you again. That's good. Shame you don't feel able to trust us in return.'

'I trust Buffy.'

'Why don't you trust me?'

I shrug. The candle on the table goes out.

Mary lights it again.

'I don't know anything about you,' she says. 'Except you've been beaten up and stripped of your clothes. And I want to help. That's it. Nothing more. I have no wish to keep you here. There's nothing to stop you running out the front door if you want to. Except perhaps some shoes. Hold on.'

She stands up.

'I'll go and find the last few things you'll need and then you'll have no reason to stay if you don't want to.'

Her face has changed. It's toughened. She walks out, Buffy following, but she's soon back. She's holding some shoes and an old coat.

'Here you are,' she says. She drops 'em in the doorway. 'Oh, and I promised a belt.'

Again she's gone and again soon back. She drops a long black belt on the pile, followed by a brown envelope.

'That's a little money in case it's useful. I don't need to be paid back. Just keep it.'

Not sure what to say or feel. She sits down again at the table.

'Thanks,' I manage.

She gives me a brief smile, then leans towards the candle. I can see her face flickering under the moving flame.

'Is there anybody you want me to ring to say where you are?' she says.

'How are you going to ring anyone when you haven't got a phone in the house?'

'How do you know I haven't got a phone in the house?'

'I've seen.'

'Not all the rooms. You haven't been in all the rooms.'

'I glanced in the doors.'

'All of them?'

'Yeah.'

'I didn't see you do that.'

'No reason why you should. I'm good at keeping an eye open. Seeing stuff.'

I have to be, Bigeyes, know what I mean? The porkers would have banged me up loads of times otherwise.

She's watching me over the flame.

'Real little survivor, aren't you?' she says.

Buffy takes a step back from me. I can feel the atmosphere change. I'm dangerous again, and there's no question whose side Buffy's on.

I look back at Mary.

'I checked in the rooms on my way here. You went on ahead and left me to follow. So I glanced through the doors.'

'And you saw no phone?'

'Yeah.'

'What else did you see?'

'Stuff that doesn't look like it belongs to an old woman.'

'Like what?'

'Like a train set.'

'It's my grandson's.'

'You haven't got a grandson.'

'How do you know?'

'I just do. I can tell when someone's zipping me over.'

'What does that mean?'

'Work it out for yourself.'

She moves back from the flame but the light goes on dancing over her face. She frowns suddenly.

'You're very sharp. And you're right about the phone. There isn't a phone in the house. But you don't know I haven't got a mobile.'

'Yes, I do.'

'You can't. You haven't looked in my bag.' She gives a start. 'Have you?'

I wait, deliberately, then, 'No, I haven't been through your bag. I don't need to. I just know you haven't got a mobile.'

'Instinct? Is that it? Or are you psychic?'

There's a hard tone in her voice now.

'Call it what you like,' I say.

She looks down at the flame. I can smell the scent from both candles. One's lemon, the other's lavender. She speaks again.

'Why would I offer to ring someone on your behalf if I didn't think I could do so?'

I don't answer. I'm looking at Buffy. She's all tensed up like she's going to snap at me any moment. I've got to get out of here. Whatever it is about this old girl, there's something not right. She's helped me out of a spot and she's probably harmless but I don't trust her. And anyway, I've got places to go. I can't stay here.

'I was going to go out to the phone box,' she says. 'There's one just down by the towpath.'

'I know.'

'I was going to use that.'

'It's been vandalized.'

'Oh.'

She looks surprised and for the first time I almost believe her. But I've still got to go. Something's all wrong here. Buffy's quivering, her eyes fixed on me. Mary's watching too.

I stand up.

'Got to go.'

'OK.'

'Thanks for the clothes.'

'It's OK. Try the other things on.'

I put on the belt, shoes, coat.

'Do they fit?' she says.

'They're OK.'

I pick up the envelope, glance inside. Hundred quid.

'Very generous.'

'It's no problem.'

'I don't need it.'

'You can't use a hundred pounds?'

'I can use it but I don't need it.'

'You've got plenty of money?'

'I got to go.'

'All right.'

I drop the envelope on the table. Buffy bares her teeth.

'Easy,' says Mary.

It takes me a moment to realize she's not talking to the dog.

'What did you think I was going to do?' I say.

'I don't know.' The old woman's watching me closely. 'That's why I'm scared of you.'

I look down, look up.

'I don't want you to be scared of me.'

She says nothing. I move towards the door, stop. There's that feeling again. Something's still wrong, something else. Can't work out what it is. But Buffy's restless again and this time it's not cos of me.

'What is it?' says Mary.

I don't answer. I'm listening. All I can hear is the hiss of the candle on the shelf as the wax runs down. Otherwise silence, in the house, around the house. But it's still not right. I've felt this before, many times, and I'm never wrong.

'There's someone near the house,' I say.

'What makes you say that?' says Mary.

Before I can answer, the kitchen window shatters and a brick comes flying through.

I see two figures standing outside.

Men. Hard-looking gobbos. Never seen 'em before.

Buffy's barking her head off. Mary's on her feet, pushing me into the hall. She doesn't need to. I want to wig it out of here quick as blink.

'Run!' she says.

I run for the front door. Yeah, yeah, I know what you're thinking. I ought to stick it out with her. Bollocks. I'm racing down the hall. Another crash from the kitchen window, then a shadow in the front door.

Stop, think, but there's no time.

The glass in the front door smashes and there's a third gobbo looking in. Big grunt of a guy. I hear Mary's voice behind me.

'The window! Main bedroom! Climb out and run!'

I'm already racing past her. Another crash from the kitchen, more shattering glass, then a bang on the front door. The grunt's got something big pounding against it.

Buffy's charging about, still barking. Voices from the kitchen, heavy voices. The gobbos are climbing through the window. Here's the main bedroom.

Stop at the door, look back.

Mary's just standing in the hall. She hasn't moved. Buffy's stopped too, right beside her, stopped barking even, like they're waiting, just waiting for what's coming. She shouts at me suddenly.

'Run!'

I run through the main bedroom, open the window. No figures on the outside, just the dronky back garden of the bungalow and beyond that the canal. I climb out, tumble onto the hard ground, jump up and run towards the fence.

Voices inside the house, men's voices shouting, roaring. No sound of Mary, just Buffy barking again. A crash from the other end of the house. The grunt's almost smashed in the front door.

Stop, think, breathe.

I know, I know. Don't keep telling me, OK?

I creep back to the house, slow, slow. Don't ask me what I'm going to do cos I haven't got a clue. Probably no use anyway. What can I do against those gobbos?

But I can't leave the old girl. I know she was lying to me but she did rescue me. She did give me the clothes. I'm trembling. Why's it gone so quiet? Even Buffy's gone quiet. No voices, no banging and crashing, nothing.

I'm close to the window now, right by it. Still silence.

Then the gunshot.

I freeze. I'm clutching the window, shaking. Silence again, dead silence. Inside, outside, like the world's gone still.

Bang!

A second gunshot.

And I'm gone. Over the lawn, over the fence, out to the road, off towards the industrial estate. Don't try and stop me. Waste of time yakking in my head. I don't care what's right or wrong. Mary's dead. That's all I know. Buffy too, probably.

I'm wigging it out of here.

Don't look back, don't stop. I hate this road. Empty bloody thing, craggy fence, scrawny fields either side. Nowhere to hide if those gobbos come out. They'll see me straight away. They know there's a witness. They saw me inside the house.

But there's no other way out of here. I'm not going back along the canal. That's even more exposed. If I can just get to the industrial buildings, I'll be all right for a bit.

Hundred yards, fifty, twenty. I'm panting but I'm nearly there.

GJB Electronics UK. Am I pleased to see you? Round the side of the building, over the lorry park, down to the refuse bins, through them and on to the low wall. Over and on to the next site. Down the side of the tyre depot, past the welder's, on round the back of the builder's yard.

Stop, lean against the wall, breathe, think.

Can't think. Keep seeing pictures of Mary. I was hard on her. She was lying but she was helping me. She offered me money. She'd have let me take it. Those women joggers wigged it but Mary stopped and helped me.

Don't look at me like that. I feel bad enough already. I don't need you dumping guilt on me as well.

Mary. I keep seeing those eyes, keep seeing those candles glowing on her face.

Get up. Come on, get up.

I get up. Don't feel better but I'm on my feet and I know what I'm going to do. I can't do anything for Mary but I might be able to shunt those gobbos.

Think. Come on, think. Get your brain working again.

Over the builder's yard, out the other side. That's better. Moving's good, thinking's good. Over the fence, down to the end of the estate. Getting dark now. City's all bright but it's dark round here. Those lights might as well come from Mars.

There's the phone. I'm just praying no one's smashed it up. Looks OK. Check it out. Dialling tone's fine. Breathe, think, calm down. Another breath. I hate talking to porkers. Another breath. Right, do it.

Nine . . . nine . . . nine . . .

Quick answer. Woman's voice, nice voice, kind of warm, kind of friendly. Sort of person you'd want to talk to. Only I can't do it. Don't look at me like that. I just can't do it, OK? She's talking again, asking me which service I want.

I put the phone down. I put the bloody phone down.

Got to think, got to be alone, got to be somewhere safe. Just as well I know the very place. But it means I've got to let you in on a secret.

Now listen, cos I'm going to tell you something nobody knows and I'm not sure I can trust you. No, I'll put that another way. I DON'T trust you. All right? I don't trust you one little bit.

Why should I? I don't even know you. I've told you my favourite name but that's all. You're just hanging around. You maybe thought I was a bit spitty not trusting Mary. I wasn't being spitty. If you've seen what I've seen in fourteen years, you'd learn not to trust. And you wouldn't want to spend time talking on the phone to porkers either.

How do I know you're not going to shunt me? Well, I'll take a chance on you. I need some company tonight. But you keep what I tell you to yourself, OK? Right, here's the thing.

Most kids like me don't last. They slap it for a bit, sleeping rough, getting cold, then before they know it, they're starving, shivering, drugged out. If they're not banged up by the porkers, then some other gobbos are using 'em, know what I mean?

Or they're dead.

Or they're back home with Mummy.

None of that applies to me. Why? I told you before—I'm different. I don't get many nights when I have to slap it. Five nights out of seven, I'm snugged out and nobody owns me. Cos nobody knows I'm there.

How do I do it? Simple. Simple and tricky at the same time.

First you got to know the city. This girl takes some knowing and she's fickle. She changes all the time. Sometimes she's a queen, sometimes she's a bit of a dingo. And she's big, big, big.

That can be good or it can be scary. Depends on her mood. She can love you one minute, bite your head off the next. I don't always like her. But I do respect her and I'll tell you this—I know her.

I know her like nobody in the world knows her. I told you earlier that I see things no one else can. Well, sometimes it's like I see everything that happens.

You smirking at me?

BLADE

Don't shake your head. I can see you smirking at me. Well, stop, cos I'm telling the truth. I see stuff and that's cos I know the city, and cos I watch. It starts with watching. You got to take your time and see how things work.

Took me years to learn it. When I was little—I mean dead little and those ticks still had their hands on me—I couldn't manage it. I couldn't move cos of them and even when I broke free, I was spinning like a top.

But I told you—I see things, and I learn quick. And the first thing I learned was how to watch. I watched the city. I watched her day and night, just like I do now. You got to do it all the time so you don't miss anything. It's when you're not watching that you get caught.

So you stay one step ahead, always one step ahead.

First thing I noticed when I started watching the city—really watching, I mean—was how many people don't live in their homes. Yeah, I know—most people do. I'm not interested in them. It's the ones who don't that matter. You got to be patient to find out who they are.

But it's worth it. If you watch long enough, you find there's snug empty homes all over the city. Most nights I'm spoilt for choice. Sometimes, like I say, there's nowhere and I have to slap it like any other duff.

But it's rare. Tonight I could name three places to snug out. So we'll take the best.

Come with me and I'll show you a bit of my world. Just a bit, mind. Don't get any ideas.

But I need to talk. I need to get my mind straight. I'm messed up. First the stuff with Trixi, then Mary and that crazy dog. So you can stick around with me a bit longer.

But don't lag behind. I can't talk if you're behind me. Right, see that light over there? Other side of the wall? It's a little burger kiosk. Guy called Abdel runs it with his son. Look to the right. Entrance to the park. We're going that way.

Not into the city. We'll keep away from that. We're heading for the outskirts.

Walk, walk, walk.

Walking helps, helps you think, and when you don't want to think, it helps that too. Sometimes I walk thirty miles in a day, sometimes more.

Walk to think, walk to forget. Doesn't always work but it can help.

Here's the wall. No point going the long way round. Climb over, drop down, check around. Gangs use this park sometimes. Trixi and those other trolls hang about here, and all kinds of other nebs. So keep your eyes open.

Walk, walk. Into the park, through the trees, over the football pitch.

Watch. Keep watching. That's how you stay alive. I know Trixi got me earlier but that should be a warning to you. If I can get caught, anyone can.

So watch. Trixi's the least of your worries round here.

Walk on, leave the football pitch, through the other gate, out of the park. See the lights to the left? City's waking up. Different energy at night. Can you feel it? She's beautiful when you're on the outside looking in. I'm feeling better for walking.

Not right though. Not right at all. Keep seeing Mary's face.

I need to snug out. I need it badly. But it's not far now.

Past the allotments, past the petrol station. More allotments. Houses thinning out, see? Keep to the side of the road. Keep close to the front gardens.

Walk small. We can't use this place if anyone sees us. We'll have to use one of the other snugs. But we should be all right. They're mostly old nebs living round here and the curtains are drawn across. Just a few more yards and . . .

Welcome to the snug.

Now do exactly what I do. Keep your eyes open and above all keep quiet. If you give me away, we're finished. You and me, I mean. Mess up one of my snugs and we part company.

Right, keep low. Every snug's different but the rules are the same. You go in unseen, you stay in unseen, you come out unseen, and nobody—NOBODY—ever knows you've been in there. Least of all the owners. So watch, copy and learn.

First thing with this snug, we go round the back. It's an old couple owns this house. Dotty old nebs. She's sixty-one, he's seventy-two. I watched 'em for a year or more before I decided to use their place. Like I told you, you got to keep watching. I'm watching loads of places and loads of people all the time. That's how I know what's going on.

The best people are the ones who aren't like me. Where I notice everything, they notice nothing. Take the nebs who live here. I know their names, their dates of birth, their hobbies, their histories. I know the names and addresses of their families and friends, the guy they use to do their plumbing, the kind of food they like.

What do they know about me?

Nothing. They don't even know I exist. And they don't know that ten or more times in the last six months I've been snugging out in their house.

How do I find out all this stuff about them? Easy. From the things they leave around the place. It's all there for you and they never know you know, as long as you're careful and make sure everything—EVERYTHING—is exactly as it was when you leave as when you went in.

Touch stuff, yeah, but put it back exactly as it was.

Like I say, the best snugs to use are the ones owned by people who don't notice stuff. I could probably move things in this house and the dear old nebs wouldn't notice when they got back.

But I don't take that risk. I'm careful. I'm good at what I do. That's why I'm still here. That's why I'm in control.

OK, round the back. See that little shed? Bottom of the garden? They don't use it for much. Couple of spades and a lawnmower. Bits and bobs. Come round the back of it and I'll show you something.

See that old stone? Lift it up. Presto! Back door key to the house. Well, copy of the key. These nebs are a sweet pair. When they're in the house, they leave the back door unlocked and the key still in the lock. Then they sit in the front room and watch TV.

When they go away every weekend to stay with their son and his family, they lock the back door and put the key in the kitchen drawer. By the time I'd worked out where they were going every Friday, I'd got a copy made of the key.

Lovely old couple. Regular as clockwork in everything. Taxi picks 'em up at ten in the morning every Friday. Same cab company, usually same guy. He gets out and puts their cases in the boot.

The old girl says, 'How are you?' and they have a little natter while the old boy struggles into the cab. Anyone with a bit of patience and a decent pair of ears can find out that they're off to the station to go and stay with their boy and they won't be coming back till Sunday.

If the driver was a crook, there'd be trouble, not just for the old nebs but for me. But he's not so I guess we're all lucky. Anyway, come on in but keep to the right. You got to stay out of the sight-line from next door. Keep this side of the path and they can't see you. And don't make a sound or knock anything.

Let's go.

Key in the back door. See? Turns cute. Open the door, slow. It used to squeak a bit but I put some oil on the hinges last time I snugged out here. Close the door. Lock it. Take the key out.

Keep still, listen. Make sure everything's OK. We should be all right. With some of the snugs you need to ring to make sure the nebs have gone. Can't do that here. You're exposed on the front door step and the neighbours can see you.

But it's OK. I know the signs. No key in the back door. See? It's in the kitchen drawer like I told you. Curtains in the front room drawn back. No lights on in the house. All quiet. They're not here.

But we'll give each room an eyeball. Always do that. Check everything. Make sure we're safe.

Right, shoes off. Park 'em out of sight behind the tumble-dryer. Walk slow.

Rule one—never move fast in the darkness. Rule two—don't switch anything on, especially the lights, not unless I say it's all right.

Sometimes it's OK. All the snugs are different. Some of 'em you can switch lights on, listen to the radio, watch TV, other stuff. Sometimes you can have a bath or a shower, cook a meal, whatever. As long as you clean up afterwards so it's exactly like it was before, nobody ever knows.

Here you can't do too much. All the rooms except one have got a window and any nebs outside'll see the light easy. Same thing with noise. You got to be really careful here. Next door'll hear if you play something too loud.

But I don't come here for that anyway. Not this

snug. I mean, we'll put the radio on later really low so I can hear if there's any news about Mary. But that's the only thing I want the radio for. Like I say, I don't come to this snug for the radio or the TV.

I come here to read.

Cos these old nebs are bung-crazy about books.

I didn't use to like 'em but I really got into 'em now. Sometimes, when I'm off my head, it's books that calm me down.

Not always. When I'm getting flashbacks, nothing can sort me. But I still like books and these two have got hundreds.

Come on. We need to check out downstairs.

Nice and quiet, nice and dark. I love the darkness. You can wrap up in it. It's like a warm bed, and there's an even warmer bed waiting for me upstairs.

All clear down here. See all the books? When's the last time you saw that many in one place? They can't possibly read 'em all.

Back down the hall. Mind the pictures. Don't knock 'em off-line.

Up the stairs. Walk quiet, just in case.

Stop on the landing, look around.

More books, see? Shelves groaning. Books, books, books. Same in all the upstairs rooms. They've even got books in the bathroom. Look at this one. I tried it last time I came here.

Superman and the Will to Power.

I thought it'd be comics but there's no pictures at all, just a load of stuff about a gobbo called Nietzsche. Never mind, try this one.

Treasure Island.

Now that's what I call a story. I've read it six times, maybe more. Every time I come here, I read a whole book. Non-stop, every word. I read fast. Book a night, no problem. Other snugs have got books too and sometimes I don't have to read in the dark.

But it doesn't make any difference.

As long as I can see the words, I'm all right.

Only I didn't finish *Treasure Island* last time I came here. I was tired. I had to sleep. I just got to the bit where Jim Hawkins is hiding in the apple-barrel and listening to the pirates plotting, and then Long John Silver says, 'Fetch me an apple,' to one of his mates, and at that moment . . .

Sssh!

Don't make a sound, Bigeyes.

There's someone by the back door.

Keep still. Stay behind me on the landing. Let me peep round the side of the stairway.

Nobody. I can see all the way down to the back door. But somebody's out there. Don't ask me how I know.

Sssh!

Footsteps in the garden, a shadow coming towards the door. Stops. I can see him now. It's the grunt I saw outside Mary's front door. Ugly looking gobbo. I can see him better from up here than when I was close to him at Mary's. He can't see me on the landing, not with this shadow.

But he's not looking anyway. He's staring at the door. He's bending down, fiddling with something. Shit, he's picking the lock.

Quick—and quiet!

Down the landing to the end, open the little door, up the other stairway. Freeze! A rattling noise. Can you hear it? Well, I can. He's not in yet but he soon will be. Top of the stairway, push open the door.

Lumber room.

Nothing else for it. Hide in one of those big card-board boxes. Not the tea-chests. Too obvious. Try the box in the corner.

Can't hear anything downstairs.

That's even more dangerous. We're top of the house now. We wouldn't hear much down there. He might be in, he might not.

Listen.

Silence. Deep silence.

I just know he's in.

We got to be silent too. And not a sound getting into that box.

Climb in. Slow, slow, ease in. Now then—pull the lids down.

Don't breathe.

Just wait and listen.

Not a sound downstairs, not a breath, not a whis-per. But he's in. I know it. He's in and he's looking for me. There's no way this is coincidence. I see the grunt through Mary's front door. He sees me. Him and the gobbos break in and shoot Mary. See me running away.

A witness.

Grunt sees which way I go and follows. Probably got his two mates with him in the street. I must have missed 'em on the way here.

We're in the grime, Bigeyes.

I'm telling you. We're in the grime.

Footsteps. Hear that? Down on the landing.

They've stopped. No, they're starting again. He's taking his time, getting his bearings, checking every room.

No sign of a light. Not using a torch, not yet anyway. He can use one in this room. The only room in the house with no window. The place I come to read. Only now it's the place I'm going to get killed.

Silence again. What's he doing now? I can't work out where he is. I thought I had him underneath me in the spare bedroom. Now I'm not so sure.

Footsteps again. He's in the main bedroom, not moving so quiet now he's worked out the owners aren't here. He knows he's either alone in the house or it's just him and me.

Either way he's laughing.

He's more confident now. I can tell from the sound.

He's almost relaxed.

Click!

He's found the door to the stairway up to this room. He's opening it.

Silence.

Can't hear him but I can feel him now. Bottom of the stairway, looking up to the top. I just know he's looking up. He's looking up and listening out for some clue that I'm here. In a moment he'll make his way up, and as soon as he sees there's no window in the lumber room, he'll put the light on, or switch a torch on.

And I'm finished.

Footsteps on the stairway.

Slow, slow, quite heavy now, but he's happy. If no one's up here, no one'll hear 'em. If I'm up here, he wants me to hear 'em. He wants me to be scared.

They stop.

Top of the stairway. Heavy breathing, wheezing. Door pushes open. Two more steps, three, stop.

Grunt's in the room.

Crouch down, keep low, don't make a sound. Can't see a thing, just the side of the cardboard box, all bleary with darkness. I'm quivering. There's no way out of this.

Bing!

Light goes on.

Knew he'd do that. Silence again. He's looking around, just standing there. I can picture his grunty head moving. Heavy breathing again. He's worn himself out climbing two lots of stairs but he's still too dangerous to take on. If I can wriggle past him, I might be able to wig it but if he grabs me, I'm done.

Steps again. He's walking this way.

Stops. Sound of rummaging. He's poking in the tea-chest. Growling noise, a sniffle, a sneeze, sound of wiping. Probably his sleeve against his nose. More rummaging in the tea-chest.

Stops.

Footsteps again, closer. More rummaging. He's trying some of the other cardboard boxes. Maybe this is the time to run. While he's fiddling with the other boxes, I might be able to squeeze past him and down the stairs.

Too late. The rummaging's stopped and he's moving again.

He's by the box. My box. He's breathing hard. Another sneeze, a big globby sneeze. Something grabs hold of my box, starts to fiddle with the lids, then—

A mobile rings.

He stops. I'm trembling inside the box. The lids are still in place but he's moved them just enough for me to peer up through the gap and see the side of his face. He's got a mobile clapped to his ear.

'Yeah, mate?'

He's got a voice like a sinking ship.

A pause, then he goes on.

'He's not here. Any sign of him where you are?'

Another pause.

'All right,' he says. 'Meet you there.'

He hangs up.

I want to twist my face away. The moment he looks down, he'll see my eyes watching him through the gap between the lids of the box. But he doesn't look down. He's walking back to the door. Another resounding sneeze, then the light goes off, and step, step, step down to the landing.

I don't hear the back door go, just the tramp of

his feet round the side of the house and out into the street.

And then they're gone.

I'm out of the box, down the stairs, into the main bedroom, over to the window.

There he goes down the street, not looking back, not looking at the other houses. He's talking on his mobile again.

I watch him go, watch him all the way down the street. No sign of the other two, no sign of anyone. That's why I used to like this street. There's never anybody around.

I don't feel so safe here now.

Slump down. Got to think, got to really think. They're looking for me, no question. They think I saw 'em kill Mary or whatever. Unless . . .

No, it can't be that. It can't be anything to do with that. Surely . . .

Thing is, Bigeyes, something I haven't told you—there's other people looking for me. Never mind why. All you need to know is that I got enemies. And it's big stuff, OK? Serious grime. And it goes back a long way.

Trouble is, the people I'm really scared of won't come themselves. They'll send other people. They might have sent these gobbos.

So that grunt and his two mates, they could be after me cos they think I saw 'em stick the clapper on Mary. Or they could be from the other lot, and that would be even worse. It'd mean they've tracked me to the city.

I didn't think they could do that. I didn't think anyone could do that. I thought I could just come here and play dead.

It's been working for the last three years. I've been under the radar all this time. No one in the city knows me. Not really. I mean, some people think they know me.

Trixi thinks she knows me cos she caught me working one of her streets last year, and there are others who think they know me. You still got to deal with people, even when you're playing dead. You got to buy food and do stuff.

But I'm still a ghost. I sleep where I want. I go

where I want. I call myself what I want. Even the porkers haven't touched me since I came to the city. They've never even met me. I'll be on their records from the old days but they haven't seen me since I came here. And that's how I want it.

I'm starting to feel scared. And I'm still choked up about Mary. Keep seeing pictures of her lying dead. But I can't stay slumped here.

Got to go through the ritual. Clean up, eat, drink, sleep. Stay well, stay alive.

Come on, stop shaking. Stand up, move. Out of the bedroom, through the darkness, into the bathroom. What did I tell you, Bigeyes? Books in here as well. Don't ask me what kind of plant that is. I haven't got a clue and I don't give two bells anyway.

Run the tap.

Water feels good. Face still stings from where those trolls got me but I don't care. Water's cool. I'd like to use the shower but I'm too tired and I still feel a bit vulnerable here. I didn't use to feel that way but seeing the grunt in one of my snugs has fizzed me out.

Dry my face, mop up all around with loo paper,

flush down the toilet. No traces. Nothing to show I've been here.

I'm still trembling, Bigeyes. Can't stop. Why can't I stop?

Find a book. That'll help. Might not stop it but it can't do any harm. Here's one. An old favourite.

Wind in the Willows.

I'll read that later. But eat first. Out of the bathroom, down the stairs. Keep away from the walls, Bigeyes. I told you before. You mustn't knock any of the pictures off-line. That one's already off-line. Grunt must have barged it as he went past. It wasn't me.

Straighten it, move on down the stairs.

He's left the back door unlocked.

Lock it again, move to the kitchen. Should be plenty of food here. That's why I like this place. They're not organized, these nebs. Too many books and too much food. Open that cupboard.

See?

Baked bean cans all over the place. How can two people possibly need that many baked beans? And look at all these other cans. God knows what they've got in here. Check out the bread basket.

Loads.

OK, can of baked beans, can of sweetcorn, can of button mushrooms, three slices of toast. Grill on, toast under. Saucepans on the rings. Power on.

Now this is where you got to be careful. No lights on but a little glow from the rings on the cooker. If the grunt was out in the garden now, he'd notice. We should be OK cos we're not on the sight-line from next door, but keep a watch.

And here's the other risky bit.

I'm turning on the radio, just low. But I got to hear if there's any news about Mary. Someone might have found her body.

'The headlines today. The Prime Minister has come under fire in the House of Commons over the Government's plans to increase . . . '

But there's nothing. Political stuff, new cancer drug, global warming, some actor's died. Nothing about Mary. Turn the toast, stir the food, switch off the radio.

Don't want to hear any more.

I'm choked up. What's happened to her? I keep thinking about her lying dead on the floor. I should have had the guts, should have phoned the porkers. I still could. There's a phone here.

But I know I won't.

Eat. Come on, got to eat. Plate, knife, fork. Butter the toast, scoop on the food. Smells good. Just wish I was going to enjoy it. But I can't. I'm still thinking about Mary.

Can't eat this stuff, can't eat any of it, can't eat, can't think.

Tip the food away, push it right down inside the bin, cover it over. Wash up, dry up, put everything away just as it was. Go and sleep. Tomorrow'll be better. I know what I've got to do tomorrow. But sleep first. Got to blank this all out.

Up the stairs, hold the book tight, don't let it go.

Wind in the Willows.

You know the bit I'm going to read? The bit where Ratty and Mole are in the snow and Mole suddenly smells his old home, and they go back and find it again. I'm going to read that bit before I fall asleep.

But I'm not going up to the lumber room.

I need to lie down. I need to be warm. I can read in the dark. I don't even need to see the words, not

BLADE

with this book. I know them anyway.

Top of the stairs, spare bedroom. This is where I always sleep. I roll up in that old duvet. Jump on the bed, wrap the duvet round. It's an old friend. I recognize the smell. Feels good, feels warm and dark.

Open the book.

I can see the words better than I thought. Flick through. Here's the chapter. *Dulce Domum.* It's Latin. I found out. Don't know what it means. But this is the chapter where Mole finds his old home. He follows the scent and then dives down into the ground and finds his little house.

This is where you leave me, Bigeyes. I want to be by myself now. Just me and little Mole. So get lost.

I'll see you in the morning.

Wake up. It's six o'clock.

Time to move. Got to sort this thing with Mary. And we got to get out of here before anyone sees us. Should be OK. Like I told you, they're mostly old nebs round here and it's a sleepy place. But you can't be too careful.

Check the bedroom. Tidy up. Check again.

Book back on the shelf, same place. Check round. No marks, nothing on the floor. Bathroom. Wash, dry, tidy up. Check round. Down the stairs. Not bothering with breakfast. Still can't eat, worrying too much about Mary. Got to find out what happened.

Kitchen. Check round, shoes from behind the tumble-dryer. Put 'em on. Check out the garden. All clear, all quiet. Blackbird on the fence, robin on the shed. Cold sky.

No nebs in sight.

Key in the door, open slowly, listen. Hum of traffic beyond the estate, nothing else. Push open the door, peer out. All clear. Step out, lock the door, over to the shed, key under the stone. Back down the path and round the side of the house.

Check the street. Nice and quiet. Looks almost quaint.

Why don't I feel so good?

Come on, Bigeyes. We got to move.

Down the street, past the allotments, away. On to Barton Avenue, right at the junction. Keep close, Bigeyes, don't lag. Over the railway bridge, across the field, down the alley, through the park.

All quiet, but you still got to watch. You never stop watching. Mostly it's dog walkers this time of day but there's still danger. You still got to be careful. Like I told you—I got people after me. I got to see 'em before they see me, you understand?

Keep moving. Don't slow down.

Outskirts of the city. She's waking up now. She's still a bit sleepy but she's stretching her arms and yawning. Cars, buses, cyclists. Lots of nebs out already. Students, suits, kids, shopkeepers opening up. Couple of porkers, traffic warden.

All muffins so far. Nobody dangerous. But you don't usually see the dangerous ones. That's why you watch, Bigeyes. That's why you never stop watching.

Left here and down the sliproad, through the underpass, left again. We're coming to the bungalow from the other side. Slow down a bit now.

Don't want to show ourselves.

There's the canal. See it? Over to the left. Keep back a bit. Use the parked cars to hide behind. Slowly forward. Check around. Keep checking around. I don't feel right about this place. Those gobbos could be still close. They know I've been here once. They might be watching in case I come back.

Can't see 'em. Can't see anyone.

There's the road up to the industrial estate. There's the bungalow. Looks quiet enough. No porkers outside. No police cars. Nobody at all. Couple of joggers on the canal. Lanky guy and a woman. But that's about it.

Check around. Move closer to the bungalow. Get ready to run any moment. Don't like these parked cars now. They're hiding me but they might be hiding other people.

Move on, slow, slow.

Still nobody around. Lorry moving up the road towards the industrial estate. Couple of cars and post van. Soon gone. Stop by the last parked car. Keep close to it, keep low, peer over the road.

The bungalow looks just like it did. Front door closed but the glass panel smashed in. None of the windows open as far as I can see. Wait a moment . . .

Front door's not closed. I thought it was but it's ajar. I'm sure it's ajar.

Need to get closer to be certain.

Check around. Check left, right, behind.

Over the road, stop at the front gate. Check again. Through the gate and up to the front door.

I was right. It's ajar. The grunt pounded it so hard he broke it open.

Check through. I can see good. Nobody in the hall, just glass and splinters over the carpet.

Move back. It's too risky to go in. I just know it. Round the side of the house, soft, really soft. Don't make a sound. First window. Keep to the side, edge close, peep round. The bedroom I got changed in. Nobody in there.

Next window. Bathroom. Misted glass. Next window.

Curtains drawn across.

Listen.

Not a sound inside but something's wrong about this room. Don't ask me how I know. Round the other side of the bungalow. Kitchen windows smashed in. I'm standing where the two gobbos were standing last night.

Look through.

Nothing there. Just glass all over the floor. Candle's

still on the table. It's burned right down.

No sign of Mary or the porkers or anybody. But I'm thinking about that bedroom. I don't like this, Bigeyes. I'm telling you, I don't like this. I want to run. But I feel I owe Mary something. She could be lying in there undiscovered.

She might even be still alive.

Round to the front door. I'm trembling again. I hate this. Calm down. Keep your wits about you. Move quiet. Stop by the door. Listen hard, look through again. Nobody. Push open the door, slowly. Leave it wide open. May have to run like blood.

Creep in. Splinters of glass underfoot. Step over them. Check around. Still nobody. No movement, no shadow, no breathing. But danger. I can feel it.

Whirl round.

Doorway's still clear. I can see right out to the street.

Turn back. Creep down the hall. Stop by the kitchen. Check right. Nobody there. Over to the main bedroom.

Door's closed.

Stop, listen.

Not a sound. Check back down the hall. Still

empty, still quiet. Ear to the bedroom door. Nothing, just the sound of my own breathing.

Turn the doorknob. Get ready to run.

No reaction to the sound, no shout from inside the room. But that means nothing. I push open the door, stand back.

'Shit!'

She's lying on the floor by the side of the bed, staring towards the ceiling, an upturned chair close by. But it's not Mary.

It's Trixi.

I want to run for it but my legs take me straight in. I kneel down.

'Trix!'

She's not breathing. Her eyes are glazed. There's a bruise on her head the size of a scream.

'Trix!'

A voice, but not from her.

'I'm afraid she's beyond your help.'

I whip round, jump up.

There's a guy standing behind the door, one of

the gobbos I saw peering through the kitchen window last night. He's been in the room all the time. And there's a third figure.

One of the trolls from Trixi's gang. Don't know her name. She's slumped in the far corner. Her eyes are glazed too, but she's not dead. She's choked out with fear.

The gobbo glances at her.

'Lost her voice, poor thing. They're all the same, these kids. Think they're tough because they're part of a gang and the first sign of violence they fall apart.' He bellows at her. 'Don't you!'

She doesn't answer, just shivers. She's white. She's all closed up. I'll get no help from her. The gobbo closes the door, looks over at me.

'I was hoping you might come back.'

I look around. Got to be something I can do.

'There's nothing,' says the man, watching me. 'Nothing you can do.'

'What do you want?'

'You, my friend. I thought that was obvious.'

'What for?'

'Because of who you are.'

'And who am I?'

'Oh, we're clever, are we? Quick-witted? I was told you might be.'

'You don't even know me. I'm just some kid who's walked in. You never even seen me before.'

'You match the description well enough, even allowing for the changes over the last three years.'

I glance at the girl. If only she'd do something. With two of us we might be able to confuse him or something. He hasn't jumped on me yet and he could have done. If it was just murder he wanted, he'd have rubbed me out by now.

Like he did Trixi.

I glance at her. She's gone. No doubt about it. I'm guessing he smashed her over the head with that chair. I look back to the gobbo.

'What did you kill her for? What's she done?'

'Who said I killed her?'

He's zipping me over. I know he killed her. I shout at the troll.

'Did he kill her?'

No answer. Don't think she's even heard me. She's just huddled there. Gobbo shakes his head.

'You can take that as a no.'

'I'll take it as a yes.'

He's not even listening. He's talking into a mobile.

'I've got him in the bungalow. How long will you be? OK, see you in five minutes.'

He hangs up, gives me a little smile. I shout at the troll.

'Throw me your knife!'

Still nothing from her, not even a look. Gobbo speaks.

'I think that might be hard for her. I seem to have acquired it myself. When we had a little scuffle.'

He pulls out a knife, gives me another smile.

That's it, Bigeyes. I didn't want to touch her but there's nothing else for it. I'm into Trixi's pockets and here's her knife first go. I pull it out, flick it open, turn back.

Gobbo's stiffened. He's watching me close. He should have jumped while I was looking away. Why hasn't he? He's wary, wary of a kid. But he's talking confident.

'That's my boy! Now I know you're who I thought you were.'

Say nothing. Watch. Wait. Choose the moment. There'll only be one.

'You're the boy they call Blade,' says the man.

'You're looking for someone else.'

'The boy who's a wonder with a knife.'

'You're looking for someone else. I never heard of a kid called Blade.'

'But you're a wonder with a knife. Anyone can see that. Look at the way you're handling it. Like you could just throw that knife and hit anything you wanted.'

'You better watch out, then, Scumbo.'

'Oh, I'm watching out.'

He is, too. He's talking big but his eyes are fixed on me. I can read his mind, Bigeyes. He's thinking the kid's got one shot with that knife. It could be lethal or he might miss. Too risky to take a chance so wait till the other gobbos get here.

Sound of an engine outside the bungalow.

Gobbo gives me a gloaty look.

'We're going to take you to see some old friends. They're looking forward to catching up with you again. You'll have lots to talk about.' He glances at the girl. 'Unfortunately we're going to have to silence our companion. But we can't take any risks, I'm afraid. I'm sure you both understand.'

Engine falls quiet. Crunch of car doors, two of 'em. The other gobbo and the grunt probably. Footsteps on the path. Got to do something, got to act now.

But the troll moves first.

She takes me by surprise, and the guy by the door. She's on her feet. She's choked out of her wits but she's making herself move. She yells at me.

'Throw the knife at him!'

Footsteps in the hall. I raise my arm to throw the knife. Gobbo does the same with his but I can see he's not comfortable. He's holding it all wrong. He can cream a knife off a girl but he's got no idea how to throw it.

But there's no time for either of us to throw.

The girl jumps across the bed, picks up the chair and hurls it at the window. The glass shatters and the chair carries through into the garden.

Gobbo shapes to throw again but the door opens behind him and knocks him down. I see the grunt glaring through at me from the hall.

'There he is!' he bawls.

Girl grabs me by the arm.

'Out the window!' she shouts and dives through the gap. I'm right behind her, still holding the knife. We roll over the grass and scramble to our feet.

'Run!' she says.

We're tearing across the garden. Over the fence, into the road. My arm's got a gash from the jagged glass. Footsteps behind us. I'm following the girl and she's running like the wind. If she was frozen before, she's fizzing now.

She's heading for the canal.

Don't know if it's a good idea. Don't know anything any more. But there's no time to think. Got to run. Got to run, run, run.

So we run.

Onto the bridge, over the canal, down to the towpath. Left or right? She goes right, towards the city. I don't argue, just follow. We're haring down the towpath. Nobody about but she's made the right decision. We need people around us and the city's the place.

Check behind.

No sight of the grunt but the two gobbos have reached the bridge.

'Keep up!' says the girl.

I'm struggling. She's fast and I'm not. But we've got a head start on the gobbos and if we get to the end of the towpath quick enough, we should lose 'em. Girl glances back.

'Shit!' she says.

I see what she means. They're quicker than I thought. They're racing down after us, much quicker than me, quicker than the troll even. But here's the end of the towpath. We push through the gate.

'Head for Meadway Drive,' I say.

'What for?'

'There's a building site, shops, people. We need people round us.'

She cuts off towards Meadway Drive. The gobbos are much closer now, just a few yards from the gate but we're over the street and tearing down Meadway Drive. There's the building site. Plenty of guys there already, and lots of nebs down the shopping parade, even some school kids. Look behind.

The gobbos have stopped. One's talking on a mobile. I touch the troll on the arm.

'They've stopped.'

'I've seen,' she says.

She carries on running and I do the same. She's right. We got to get well clear of them, got to put some distance between us.

We run on. I'm tired out now and she must be too, but I can see from her face she's still choked out. She's probably thinking of Trixi, and so am I.

I didn't like her, Bigeyes. I hated her. But I didn't want to see her dead, any more than I wanted to see Mary dead. If she is dead. I still don't know what happened to the old girl. Maybe the gobbos dumped her somewhere.

Some time or other I'm going to have to decide what to do. But one thing I know for certain.

I don't want to get mixed up with this troll. I got enough to think about, especially with these gobbos. They used my name. They're from the past, and that means trouble.

Playing dead hasn't worked.

The last thing I need is this troll hanging round.

I've survived by staying alone. That's the only way to ride the dream. Stay alone. Then no one can touch you.

She's slowing down. I'm glad of that. I'm bombed out. I need to rest.

We're closer to the city centre now. Loads of nebs around. No sign of danger but I'm checking about me real cute. Cos everything's changed now. I've got to watch more carefully than ever, and I've got to decide about this troll. But she's got ideas of her own.

'This way,' she says.

She's heading down one of the alleyways towards the dockyard. Not a place I'm keen on. But at least the gobbos shouldn't find us down here.

I follow. Don't want to, Bigeyes. I want to split. But I've got to talk to this girl. I've got to find out what happened. And she might know about Mary.

But I don't like following other people. I like to go where I know I'm safe.

'Where are we going?'

She doesn't answer. I'm thinking about the other trolls now. I don't want 'em in my face again. But she's not looking for them. She's pulled round into a side alley.

I've seen this place before. Doesn't run through to anything, just a little cul de sac where drunks or druggies hang out. Sometimes you find the odd duff sleeping under a newspaper.

No one here now.

She slumps down, back against the wall, turns to the side.

And she's throwing up.

I can't deal with this, OK? I can't deal with it. I know she's choked out. I know she's lost her mate. But I can't be dealing with this. I've got to think of myself.

Don't look at me like that. I've got to think of myself. You understand? It's how I survive.

I'VE GOT TO THINK OF MYSELF.

I'm still standing there, looking down. She's gobbed all over the ground and now she's retching with nothing coming up.

Don't know what to do.

What do I do, Bigeyes? Tell me what to do.

I bend down.

'You all right?'

She doesn't answer. Don't blame her. It was a stupid question.

She's stopped retching now. Pulls out a paper handkerchief, wipes her mouth, stands up, looks at me, anger in her eyes. Walks past me, stops a few yards away, slumps down again. Can't work this girl out.

'I'm moving away from the sick,' she says.

'Oh.'

Silence.

She's dropped her head, like she doesn't want to look at me. Obviously wants me to go. I start to walk past her.

'Stay,' she says.

I stop, look down. She lifts her head just enough for me to see her eyes. They're still angry.

'Stay,' she says.

I sit down next to her. She lights a cig, takes a few drags, offers it to me.

'No, thanks.'

'Clean-living kid, are you?'

I don't answer.

'What did you do with the knife?' she says.

'I closed it up while we were running.'

'Where is it?'

'In my pocket.'

'Give it to me.'

I look at her. Don't like those eyes. They scare me. She's out of her mind right now. She holds out her hand.

'Give it to me.'

'What you going to do with it?'

'I ain't going to stick it in you if that's what you're worrying about.'

I give her the knife.

She looks at it, flicks open the blade, starts crying. It makes her look young. She must be about sixteen like the other trolls in the gang. She looks like a little kid now.

But the tears don't last. She wipes them away, savagely, and then she's sixteen again. She stares at the knife, runs a finger along the edge.

'So that's your name, is it?' she says.

She looks up at me.

'Blade?'

'My name's Jonny,' I say.

'That guy called you Blade.'

'He was mixing me up with someone else.'

'He said you know how to handle a knife.'

'I told you. He was mixing me up with someone else.'

'You looked like you can handle a knife. When you was holding it. You looked like you've used a knife before.'

'I was just pretending. Trying to scare him.'

'So you're called Jonny?'

'Yeah.'

'And what are you called when you're not lying?'

'Jonny.'

'I'm calling you Blade.'

I don't want her to, Bigeyes. I don't want that name getting around. I told you the name but you're the only one I've told it to since I came to the city.

It's a name from my old life.

It's the name Becky gave me so it's special. Cos Becky was special. I don't want this troll using it. I look back at her.

'So what's your name?'

'Becky.'

Shit, Bigeyes, this is going from bad to worse. And she's not zipping me over. She's telling the truth.

I can always tell. She's called Becky. She's bloody called Becky.

'I'm calling you Blade,' she says again.

'I don't give two bells what you call me.'

'Two what?'

'Never mind.'

'You talk funny.'

'I talk like I talk.'

She's not listening. She's crying again. She's like loads of things all at once now. Angry, sad, frightened, defiant. A little kid and a fighting troll.

And she's still holding the knife.

I'm watching it. Whatever she said about not sticking it in me, I'm watching that knife.

'Becky?'

Feels funny saying her name. She doesn't answer, just goes on crying those angry tears.

'Becky? What happened in the bungalow?'

She's looking round at me. Eyes wet, cheeks wet. I'm telling you, she's right on the edge. I've got to watch everything she does. She wipes her eyes with her sleeve, glares at me, answers.

'We went in, me and Trix. It was a test.'

'What kind of test?'

'A test for me. To see if I had the bottle.'

'For the gang?'

'Yeah. I'm on the outside, right? I'm not one o' them. I ain't proved myself. They think.'

It sounds right. I recognized the other five trolls. Didn't recognize this one. And she hung back a bit when they sorted me on the towpath. Just a bit.

She still got in a couple of kicks.

'So it was a test?'

'Yeah. Trixi's been watching the bungalow. She's wanted to break in for ages.'

'What for? There's nothing much in there.'

'It's not about nicking stuff.'

'So what is it about?'

'It's about doing some damage. She don't like the people who live there. The guy mouthed her off once for making a noise in the street. His wife joined in too. And their son's a greasy little snipe. So it's personal.'

I'm listening hard, Bigeyes. A guy, she said. A wife, a son. Nothing about old Mary.

'So what happened?' I say.

'Trix told us she'd seen 'em leave the house, all

packed up like they was off on holiday. And we was all set to go in the next day. But we found some old girl with a dog hanging round there. So we had to wait.'

'Who was she?'

'Don't know.'

'Then what?'

'Day after we done you on the towpath, Trix tells me we're going in, just her and me. Says the old woman's gone and I got to break in with her. Says I got to nick some stuff and mess the place up but not leave no prints or nothing.'

'Why just you? Why not the other girls?'

'Cos she knows I'm scared, specially of the police.'

'Why?'

'None of your business.'

She gives me another glare. I'm not arguing. She's got the knife and I haven't.

'So you went in. You and Trix.'

'Yeah, only I knew something was wrong. Front door was smashed already. You seen it yourself. We just walked in. And Trix tells me to check out the spare bedroom while she does the main bedroom.'

I know where this is going, Bigeyes. I can see it already. She doesn't need to tell me any more.

'So I check out the spare room. Nothing much there. And I walk through into the main bedroom and . . .'

She seizes up again. She's not crying this time. She's shaking and retching again, and she's squeezing the hilt of the knife like she wants to crush it. I want to take it off her but I don't dare. If I touch her, she'll round on me. I just know.

'Easy,' I say.

She doesn't hear me.

'Becky? Easy.'

'Shut up!'

I shut up. Too right I shut up. Let her get through it. I don't need any more anyway. She's told me enough. I can guess the rest.

Maybe I could go. I want to go. I don't want any more of this.

But I can't move.

Don't ask me why.

She's stopped retching. She's still shaking and she's staring at me with those . . . those eyes.

She takes a slow breath.

'I walked into the main bedroom, and there's Trixi lying on the floor. I don't know why I didn't hear nothing. I mean, no scream. No . . . thump when he hit her. Maybe I was just too scared to notice stuff. I just wanted to run.'

'Then what?'

'This hand grabbed me from behind the door. I pulled out my knife but he wrenched it straight off me.'

She's gripping the knife and biting her knuckles at the same time.

'I tried to fight him but he knocked me about so hard I just . . . lost it. I crumpled up. The girls are right. I got no fight in me. Trixi wouldn't have given up. If she hadn't been hit first, she'd have given him some grief.'

'How long were you in there before I turned up?'

'Don't know. Couple of minutes, maybe more. Seemed longer.'

'Were you really scared or were you playing scared?'

'I was really scared. Then when you started answering him back, I got some bottle and went for it.'

Her face has changed again. It's got something else, something new. She's right. She's not like the other trolls. I don't know what it is. But there's something they've got that she hasn't. And something she's got that they haven't.

It's in her face right now.

I'm getting in too deep, Bigeyes. And I don't want to.

As for Mary, I don't know much more than I did. Except I was right. She doesn't live in that bungalow. I look hard at Becky.

'What are you going to do about Trixi?'

She looks angrily back at me.

'You mean, what are we going to do about Trixi?'

'No. What are you going to do about Trixi?'

'I'll leave a message with the police. But I'm not giving my name.'

'They'll come for you anyway. They must know your gang. And you got a criminal record, right?'

'I been in a bit of trouble.'

'Like what?'

'Like none of your business.'

Fair enough. Can't say I blame her. I'm keeping my secrets too.

'They'll find you,' I say. 'One of the gang'll give you away. Specially as they know you went off with Trixi. You'll be the major suspect.'

'That's why I ain't going to the police station. I'll ring 'em up and tell 'em about the men.'

'Are you going to tell 'em about me?'

She stands up suddenly.

'Depends,' she says.

'On what?'

She closes the knife and puts it in her pocket.

'Come with me,' she says.

Don't know why I'm following her. Maybe I'm worried.

OK, I am worried. I admit it. I don't like being seen, or recognized anyway. Now these nebs have turned up from the past and if this troll starts talking to the police about me, they'll start hunting as well. And they'll start looking through their records for stuff. They'll find their way right back to where I don't want 'em to go.

I got to stop her talking about me to anyone.

And that means some kind of deal. I don't know

what she wants but she wants something. I've got to find out what it is. She doesn't waste any time telling me.

'I want a doss,' she says.

She's walking fast down another one of the alleyways. We're going parallel to the dockyard, out of sight of the river. I'm struggling to keep up.

'What you asking me for?' I say.

'Cos you got somewhere to sleep.'

'You don't know that.'

'Yeah, I do.' She glances at me. 'You're smart. I can tell. You're sharp as they come. No wonder they call you Blade.'

'I told you—the guy was thinking of someone else.'

'He wasn't. He was thinking of you. You're Blade.'

We walk on down the alleyway.

'You don't know my name,' I say. 'Neither did Trixi. I never told any of your gang my name.'

She looks at me again.

'You know why Trixi called you Slicky?'

'No.'

'That was her name for you. Cos of the way you

look. She used to say you're too slick to be a street thief. You don't sleep rough. Anyone can see that. You're always clean. You've always got nice clothes on. Well, not right now.'

'Thanks to you.'

'Trix wanted to sort you proper. She didn't like you working our streets and poncing about in flash clothes.'

'They weren't flash. They were just tidy.'

'They were that, all right. You look like you come from some nice home with a nice mummy and daddy and a nice big car and a dog and a cat and lots of money.'

'Maybe I do.'

She gives a funny little laugh, kind of giggly. Makes her sound like a kid again. But the eyes soon harden and the years pile back on.

'You ain't got a home like that,' she says. 'You're a loner. You're drifting round the city same as me. You ain't got no one here. Have you?'

'None of your business.'

We reach the end of the alleyway and stop. She's looking me over again.

I can't handle this, Bigeyes. It's banging me out. I got enough to think about with those gobbos and all this stuff from the past coming back. I don't need this girl's rubble too.

'You're drifting,' she says.

'That's what Trixi told you, is it?'

'Trixi? She thought you were some jumped-up rich kid lifting wallets for fun and then going back to a nice rich home. That's why she hated you. You weren't nicking stuff cos you needed it. You were nicking stuff cos it was a laugh. All the girls thought that.'

'Except you.'

'Yeah.' She sniffs. 'Except me.'

'You might all be wrong. I might have a home. And I might not be a rich kid.'

She leans close. I move back. She stops, but she's still watching me.

'Jumpy, ain't you?' she says. 'What did you think I was going to do?'

I don't answer.

'I ain't got the knife open,' she says. 'It's in my pocket. What did you think I was going to do?'

Don't answer. Just watch. She's staring back at

me, like she doesn't know what to make of me. She straightens up.

'You're not a rich kid. And you ain't got no home. But you got a doss.'

Don't answer. Just watch.

'You got a doss,' she says. 'And I want to share it. One night, that's all. One night and I'm away. Let me stay there tonight and I won't say nothing about you to the police. I'll tell 'em about Trixi and the man and what happened. But I won't say nothing about you.'

'If I find you a doss for tonight.'

'If you find me a doss for tonight.'

'But you must have been dossing somewhere till now.'

'I have. But I can't go back there. Not now. The girls'll find me. The police'll find me.'

'They'll find you anyway.'

'Not if I'm gone.'

'Go now, then.'

She shakes her head, looks down.

'I ain't eaten for three days. The gang was giving me stuff but not much. Trixi said I had to prove myself before they'd give me anything more. I can't nick money like you do. I'm no good at it. I'd get caught first go. And now this thing with Trixi.'

She looks up again.

'The girls'll kill me. They don't like me anyway. They don't trust me. They'll think I walked out on Trixi. It won't make no difference what I tell 'em. They'll think I ran for it and let Trixi get killed. They won't even listen. And if the police get me, they'll send me back.'

'Back where?'

She says nothing but she doesn't need to. Her face is a story I don't want to read.

I don't know what to do, Bigeyes. I need this troll off my back. And how do I know she'll do what she says? She could shunt me anyway, even if I do help her. But not helping her might be a bigger risk.

'Come with me,' I say.

She shakes her head.

'You got to come with me first,' she says.

'I'm not going anywhere with you. You want a doss so you come with me. I lead the way.'

She moves so quick I don't have to time to run. One moment she's standing there, the next she's pushed me back against the wall and the knife's out and open and pricking against my throat.

'Shit, Becky! Lay off!'

'Listen.' Her voice is like distant thunder. 'We got a deal. You find me a doss for the night, and some food, and I'm out of your life in the morning. I'll come with you. I'll follow. But first you got to come with me. You got to agree to come with me.'

'What for?'

The knife moves slowly over my throat. I look all the way down it and up into Becky's eyes. They're midnight-black.

'There's someone coming with us,' she says.

We're walking on. Alleyways well behind us, docks open on the left. Lighters, barges, river slinking by. It's grey and dark, not interested in us. Too busy moving.

Same as the people. Lots of nebs round here but they're just like the river. Moving, moving, moving. I don't like coming this way. Still can't believe I'm following this troll.

She keeps looking over her shoulder, like to check I'm here.

Why am I here, Bigeyes?

I should be gone. It's hardly difficult. I could wig it easy as kiss air. She couldn't stop me with all these nebs around. I didn't even give my word. She took my look as my word but I never gave it.

Maybe I would have done if she'd pushed me. I mean, she had the knife against my throat and I'm going to agree to anything with that thing stuck there, aren't I? But it's not there now. It's back in her pocket.

So why aren't I gone?

Docks coming to an end but she's carrying on past the derricks and warehouses. River twists away here, opens up and gulps in the sea. I don't come here much. Sea scares me just looking at it. I hate the thing.

Just as well Becky's turned away from it.

She's heading right, back into the city, towards the Hedley estate. I can see the park and playing fields, the first scattering of houses. She's taking me down one of the paths that skirt the cricket pitch.

Quite a few nebs here too but they're all muffins.

Becky's fallen silent. I'm glad of that. I need to think. I need to work out what to do. I don't have to help her. Like I said, just cos she thinks I agreed doesn't mean I did agree. I don't know why I'm hesitating. I wouldn't normally. I'd just blast off out of here.

Maybe it's the name.

Becky.

Why's she got to be called that? She's nothing like my Becky. She never could be. Nobody could be. Except in the name. But maybe that's it. Maybe that's why I'm still following.

Past the cricket pitch, down Maddison Crescent, round the shopping parade, over the railway bridge, down the path alongside the track. Becky speaks for the first time since we left the alleyway.

'Blade?'

She's glancing over her shoulder, still walking. I can see her eyes, black as before.

'I'm not called Blade.'

'Yes, you are,' she says.

'What do you want?'

'You know the Hedley estate?'

Do I know the Hedley estate? Better than she does, Bigeyes, that's for sure. I know every bit of this city. I bet she doesn't.

'What about it?'

'There's a house we've got to go to.' She frowns. 'But I don't want to go in.'

'You got a problem, then.'

'I want you to go in for me.'

'That's tough cos I won't.'

She stops and turns but this time I'm ready for her. I'm already two steps back. But she doesn't come for me with the knife. She hasn't even pulled it out. She's just standing there, her mouth quivering.

I still don't trust her. Anyone can put on tears. She cried earlier but that was genuine. She was choked out over Trixi. This is different. Don't ask me how I know.

Her mouth stops moving. No tears but she's not right. She's watching me close. I'm watching her close too, as cute as I can. She could do anything right now. She doesn't move but she speaks.

'She's in a house on the estate.'

'Who?'

'Jaz.'

'Who's Jaz?'

'My daughter.'

'Your what?'

'It's short for Jasmine.'

'I don't give two bells what it's short for. How come you got a daughter? And what about—'

'There's no father.' She shrugs. 'Well, there's a father. Obviously there's a father but he's . . . ' She shrugs again. 'He's nowhere. Gone. It's just me an' Jaz. She's only three. I was thirteen when I had her. And I got to get her out of that house.'

'Then you can go and get her by yourself. It's nothing to do with me.'

She gives me this hard look.

'Get her for me and I won't tell the police about you.'

'Hold on. We had a deal. A doss and some food. Nothing about a kid.'

'I told you someone was coming with us.'

'You didn't say anything about me going to get her.'

'Well, that's the deal.'

Got to think, Bigeyes. Got to think fast. Nothing to

stop me running. But what if she does tell the police about me? I've been playing dead for three years. I've been safe under the radar and I want to stay there. Specially now those gobbos have turned up. If the porkers get onto me again, they'll make things even worse.

Not that I trust this troll to honour her word. I could fetch her kid and get them both a doss and some food, and she could still shunt me later with the police. I'll take a risk with her but there's something I need to know first.

'What's with this house? Why can't you go and get her?'

She looks me over.

'Some of the gang might be there.'

'They got a house?'

'It's not theirs. It belongs to Tammy's gran. You know Tammy?'

'I know what her nails feel like in my face.'

'She and Sash were Trixi's favourites. They both hate me. But Tammy's gran's been letting me doss there sometimes and leave Jaz with her while I'm out with the gang.'

'You been leaving your kid with an old woman you don't even know?'

'She's all right. I mean, she's stoned half the time but she's quite kind. She wouldn't do Jaz no harm. And anyway, she's never the only person there. There's always other people at the house.'

She looks away, like she wishes she hadn't just said that. I give her a prompt.

'Like who?'

She doesn't look back. She's hesitating and I know why. She knows I won't go in if it's too danger-ous. And I'm telling you—she's right.

'Like who?'

She looks back at me.

'Like . . . people. People the gang know. They just use the place to hang out.'

Use the old woman more like. I can see it clear enough.

'I can't go in,' she says. 'They'll ask questions.'

'You could tell 'em the truth. Just leave out the bit about me. You saw Trixi dead. You struggled with the guy. Threw the chair out the window. Ran away.'

'They won't believe me.'

PLAYING DEAD

'So how do you expect me to get your kid out?'

She leans closer again. I move back, keep the distance there. She stops, watching my face. She's being careful, Bigeyes. I can see that. She's trying not to push her luck. Even her voice is softer.

'You're smart,' she says. 'I told you before. You're dead smart. You ain't fast when it comes to running but your mind's quick. There's something about you. I seen your eyes moving as you walk. You don't miss nothing. You're used to staying out of sight. And you can handle yourself.'

She pulls the knife out of her pocket but doesn't flick it open.

'Take it,' she says.

I don't take it.

She reaches out and drops it in my pocket.

'Jaz'll be in one of two places. There's a little shed at the bottom of the garden. She likes to play in there. She calls it her den. Or she'll be in the lounge. She usually sits in the corner and draws.'

I'm hating the picture I've got in my head now. I can see it clear and it's fizzing me out. I don't want anything to do with it. Though I'll tell you, Bigeyes, and

I don't really understand it, but I'm starting to feel something for this kid.

Jaz, I mean.

First she's got a mum like Becky. That's bad enough. Then she's stuck with an old dunny who's stoned out of her head. Not to mention the other nebs who keep turning up.

I can guess what they're like.

'So if she's in the shed, we're lucky, and if she's in the lounge, we're not. Is that what you're saying?'

I can't believe I'm even asking this. Becky's quick with a reply.

'Yeah, but we can still get her even if she's in the lounge. We just got to watch the house and wait for our chance. If she's in the lounge on her own, you could tap on the window, get her to open it and tell her she's just got to climb out and come with you.'

'Oh, yeah, like she's going to do that with a stranger.'

'She will. I'll give you something from me, something she'll recognize. Say it's from Fairypops.'

'Eh?'

'Fairypops. We got little names for each other. She's Fairybell. I'm Fairypops.'

'This isn't happening.'

'Just say it. She'll believe you. She's dead trusting with people.'

'Haven't taught her much, then, have you?'

Becky's mouth tightens.

'I teach her what I can but she still trusts people, OK? That's how she is. Don't matter if I warn her about someone. She just trusts.'

Now it's me looking away. I can't face this troll right now. What do I do, Bigeyes? Tell me—what do I do?

Just trusts. What kind of a person just trusts? Even kids can't be that stupid, can they?

I look back at Becky.

'Let's go.'

I know this house. I knew it even when Becky was talking about it. The moment she mentioned a shed in the garden. There's a few of those round here but only one that a kid would use as a den.

I could have done with a shed like that when I was three.

Look at it. Proper little snug tucked away behind the apple tree. Not like the house. Pothole of a place, isn't it? If only the kid was in the den right now, we'd be all right. Trouble is, she's not. Don't ask me how I know.

Becky's fidgeting.

'Blade?'

'What?'

'Come on. We're wasting time. The gang's not there. It's just the old girl. See the upstairs window? She's in the bedroom.'

'I've seen her. I'm looking for the girl.'

'You got to try the shed first.'

'She's not in there.'

'You don't know. You haven't looked.'

'She's not in there.'

'The door's ajar. I can see it from here.'

'So what?'

'So she could be inside.'

I'm not answering. I can't be wasting time over this. I'm watching the house. The old dunny's still upstairs. I recognize her now. Seen her a few times round these streets. Didn't know she lived here though. Didn't know Trixi's gang use the house either. They usually work the east side.

Just shows how you got to keep watching.

Remember what I said, Bigeyes? You got to watch the city all the time, watch her as cute as you can. That's how you stay alive.

Dunny's moving. Away from the window, lost her, back again, downstairs, into the kitchen, out again, into the lounge. Slumps in the armchair. She looks bombed out.

Check around. Dronky houses, dronky gardens, dogs barking, radio on next door. Some gobbo arguing with his missus in the house opposite. Least this path's deserted and we've got a clear view of the house through the gaps in the fence.

Becky's talking again.

'Come on, Blade. Let's go.'

'I thought you didn't want to go in.'

'I've changed my mind. It's just the old girl and she's half-gone. But we'll check the shed first.'

'She's not there. I told you.'

'We'll check the shed. If she ain't there, we'll do the house.'

'No.'

I'm scowling at her. Don't know why. This is her business. She should be sorting it anyway. But there's something chipping inside my head, something about this house, something Becky won't handle.

'No,' I say.

'No what?'

'I'll do it.'

She's staring at me.

'I'm better at this than you,' I say.

'Meaning?'

'Meaning I'm better at this than you. You're not used to creeping round houses.'

'How do you know?'

'I just do. And anyway—there's something not right about the house.'

'Like what?'

'Like I don't know. But there's something not right.'

She doesn't answer.

'Wait here,' I tell her. 'I'll bring her out.'

'All right, but give her this.'

She pulls something out of her pocket. Fluffy thing, dead tiny. Gives it to me.

'Peter Rabbit,' I say.

He fits right inside my hand.

'Who's Peter Rabbit?' she says.

'Don't you ever read?'

'No, do you?'

Do I ever read, Bigeyes? If only she knew.

I put the little rabbit inside my pocket.

'So that's for Jaz?'

'Yeah. Tell her you're a friend. Tell her Fairypops is waiting outside for her.' Becky looks back at the house. 'This is stupid. I should be going in with you.'

'No, stay here and keep out of sight.'

I'm gone. Got to move now before she argues any more. Just hope she stays put. She could mess everything up. I need to keep sharp. I can't be watching for her as well.

Over the fence, across the grass, against the wall.

Listen, watch. Radio still going next door. House opposite's gone quiet but there's children shouting somewhere down the street. Bounce of a football. No sound from the dunny's house but that means nothing. Something's wrong here. Something I can't see. And Becky's right about one thing.

There's no time to waste.

Peep round the window. Dunny's still slumped in the chair. No one else in the room. Check round. No windows overlooking me from here but the front door's exposed. Round towards the back, stop by the kitchen window, check round.

Empty.

Knew it would be. The kid's upstairs but that's where the trouble is too. I can sense it. Past the kitchen, stop, check. Only one window overlooking me and that's the house on the other side of the garden but there's no one watching.

Round to the back door, stop, check again.

Nobody watching.

Thump of the football down the street, a crash, a shout, sound of laughter, running feet.

Silence.

Open the door, listen.

Not a sound inside the house.

Into the kitchen, through the hall, soft, soft. Stop

by the lounge. Door's half-open. Check through the gap. Dunny's head's drooping on her chest, cig burning in the ashtray. Up the stairs, softer now, softer than ever. This is where it gets hard. Smell of gin, dope, mould. Stop on the landing.

Check round.

Three doors, two open. Poky little bedrooms, nobody in 'em. Stop by the third. Got to be the bathroom. Why's the door closed? Ear to it, listen long.

Nothing.

She's got to be in there. Question is, who else is?

Check back down the stairs. May need to wig it fast. But I'm not going without Jaz. Don't ask me why. I don't know either. But I'm not going without her.

Squeeze the door handle, turn, push. It's not locked. Open the door, just a bit. No sound inside. Push a bit more. Door catches on something. It's someone's foot.

No one speaks.

Head round the door.

Cloud of smoke, can't see in. I make myself step over the threshold—and now it's clear. There's nebs crowded in the room.

Big, fat gobbo lying in the bath, naked as a whale. Woman slumped against the loo, two guys sprawled next to her. Needles and syringes in the basin.

Piece of paper on the floor, far corner. Pencil lying on top. A drawing, a kid's drawing. I can see it from here. A little bird.

Only there's no kid.

Suddenly the door slams behind me. One of the guys has kicked it shut. He's sitting up, drilling me with his eyes.

'Who are you?' he says.

I squeeze the fluffy rabbit in my pocket.

'Jaz's Uncle Peter.'

'Eh?'

'Jaz's Uncle Peter.'

They're all stirring now, even the gobbo in the bath. Big, misty faces. Never seen 'em before but they look like duffs off the street. Woman glances at me.

'You don't look like much of an uncle. More like a turd off the pavement.'

Gobbos all laugh.

I look round at the nebs. They're all staring at me. Guy who kicked the door shut's blocking it with his foot. Shows no sign of moving. I look into his eyes. They're still drilling me. He gives a little smirk.

'All right, Uncle Peter?'

'Where's Jaz?'

'Not here.'

'I noticed that. Where is she?'

Gobbo glances at his mates.

'Not very polite, is he?'

Another laugh. I try something different.

'Her mum's looking for her.'

'Ah, bless,' says the woman.

I look at her. She's the only one here'll tell me. But I got to handle her right.

'Cute kid, isn't she?' I say.

'Yeah.'

The woman's eyes are like dusk falling. I lean closer to her.

'Any idea where she is, darling?'

'I ain't your darling, you little gobshite.'

'Yeah, right. Any idea where she is?'

'She run out when we come in. Left her picture behind her. Try the bedroom.'

I looked in both bedrooms, Bigeyes. But maybe . . .

I step over to the far corner, pick up the drawing and the pencil, walk back to the door. The gobbo's still got his foot against it. I squeeze the fluffy rabbit in my pocket, let go, feel for the knife, lock my fingers round it.

Long time since I carried a knife for real. Even longer since I used one.

I think of Trixi and Mary, and Jaz, and then this smirking dungpot. I'm staring hard at him now, drilling him back. He's noticed the difference in my face. I can tell from his manner. His eyes are flickering downwards. He's watching my hand move inside the pocket.

He smirks again, then shifts his leg, just enough.

I open the door, listen, check round, slip out to the landing. The bedroom, she said. Which one? Could be either. Try the one on the right first.

Creep in, close the door behind me. Nobody to be seen, but I got an idea now. Down on my knees, check under the bed, and there she is—a little girl peering out.

Face like a snowdrop.

She doesn't move, doesn't scream, doesn't do anything, just looks at me with those big eyes. I give her a smile, whisper.

'Hey, Jaz. You forgot your picture.'

I hold it out to her. She doesn't take it, just looks at it, then back at me.

'Great drawing,' I say. 'You going to finish it, sweetheart?'

'Ain't got no pencil.'

'Here it is. I brought it.'

I show her the pencil.

'I can't draw under 'ere,' she says.

'Come on out, then.'

She crawls out, takes the picture and the pencil. I touch the paper.

'It's lovely, Jaz. What is it, a thrush?'

'Robin.'

'You need a bit of red for the breast, don't you?'

'Ain't got no red.'

'I'll fix that for you. Listen, guess who sent me.'

She doesn't answer. I lower my voice.

'Fairypops. She's waiting outside. Shall we go and see her? We can finish the picture later.'

I stand up, hold out my hand. Jaz gets up without a word and takes it. Then she looks at me.

'Where's Rabbit?'

'Here.' I pull him out. 'He's been missing you.'

She doesn't take him.

'Don't you want him, Jaz?'

'Got to carry the picture.'

'Do you want me to carry Rabbit?'

'Yeah.'

'OK, let's go.'

I walk her towards the door. Got to get her out of here quick. I don't like what I'm feeling in this place. But now there's another problem.

Voices downstairs.

Some of the trolls are back. Not sure how many. I can hear Tammy and a couple of others. No sound of Sash.

I open the door a fraction, listen. Voices still there, downstairs, but they've moved into the lounge. I glance back at Jaz.

'Come on.'

She doesn't argue, doesn't even look worried. Becky's right. The kid just trusts. It's scary how much she trusts. I lead her out of the bedroom, ease her to the side of the landing so we're out of view of downstairs.

Listen again.

Tammy's voice. She's talking to the old dunny, extra loud.

'Gran? You listening to me?'

Dunny says nothing. I squeeze Jaz by the hand, lean down, whisper.

'Jaz? Do you want to play a game?'

She looks up at me, says nothing, then nods. I lean closer.

'We got to be dead quiet. We got to sneak out the house without anyone seeing us or hearing us. Can you do that?'

She nods again.

'Good girl. We'll sneak out the house and go and find Fairypops. But you got to be dead quiet. Not a word, not a sound, OK?'

She nods a third time. Tammy's still raging downstairs.

'Gran, for Christ's sake! Have you seen her?'

This time a murmur back.

'Who?'

'Trixi! Has she been here?'

'No, dear.'

'What about Becky?'

Don't catch an answer this time but now there's a bang at the door, and a rush of feet, and then the door swinging open and Sash's voice.

'She's dead!'

An explosion of shouts. They're all gabbling at once but Sash is pouring out the story.

'She's in that bungalow by the towpath. She must have took Becky with her. I went in and found her in the bedroom. She's been smashed over the head.'

'What about Becky?' says Tammy.

'Not there. But listen.'

Sash is breathing hard. I can hear it from upstairs. She goes on.

'I seen her. She didn't see me but I seen her. On my way to the bungalow, I seen her running down Meadway Drive. She was running towards the docks. And you know who she was with?'

'Who?'

'Slicky.'

There's a buzz from downstairs. The old dunny's

trying to speak, something about calling the police. The trolls aren't listening and neither am I. I'm looking about me, trying to find a way out.

They're still in the lounge. If we go down now, we might just be able to slip out without being seen. Cos in a moment they're going to come and check for Jaz. They'll know Becky's got to come back for her. I give her another whisper.

'Ready, Jaz?'

But now the bathroom door opens.

The gobbo from the bath's standing there, still naked, dripping water all over the floor. He slopes out onto the landing and stands there, swaying. I pull Jaz closer but his eyes don't even notice us. The woman steps out too, then the other two gobbos. The naked guy bellows down the stairs.

'Can you people stop that damned infernal row?'

Got a posh mouth for a duff and it's the last thing we need. Tammy's already out of the lounge and shouting up at him.

'Get out of here! We've told you before! Get out!'

In a minute she'll be up the stairs and then she'll

see us. I glance back towards the bedroom. There's just a chance . . .

The naked guy's answering back in that same plummy voice.

'We're here by right, young woman. Your grand-mother was kind enough to invite us.'

I lean down to Jaz. She hasn't moved, hasn't said a word, hasn't let go of my hand. Her face is watch-ing mine. I whisper.

'Come with me.'

Into the bedroom, slow, soft. Check behind, but nobody's watching us. The nebs are shouting down the stairs and the trolls are shouting up.

I close the door, let go Jaz's hand, top sheet off the bed, bottom sheet, tie 'em together, tie the end to the bedpost, open the window, throw out the sheet.

This might not work.

But it's got to.

'Jaz, listen.'

She's looking up at me with those eyes.

'Jaz, you got to do what I say. I'm going to sit you on my shoulders and you're going to hang on to my head. And we're going to climb down to the garden. Can you do that?'

She nods.

I can't believe this kid. You just say something and she does it.

More shouts. Tammy's getting heated up. It's time to go. I test the end of the sheet, check out the window.

'Now, Jaz.'

Lift her on my shoulders, legs either side of my head. She's as light as a feather. Just as well. She's got the drawing pushed against my face.

'Can we leave the picture behind, Jaz?'

'No.'

'OK.'

No point arguing.

'Hold on tight.'

She holds on, her hands and the picture clasped over my eyes. I can hardly see but I can feel my way. Leg over the window-frame, hands on the sheet, other leg over the edge. Sheet's holding fine. Now down, easy, easy. Sheet's holding, girl's holding. We're on the ground.

'Good girl.' I put her down. 'Let's go and find Fairypops.'

I take her hand, lead her to the back of the house. Voices still shouting inside. Check out the garden. On the other side of the fence I can see the top of Becky's head. She's moved round towards the shed at the bottom and she's seen us. She's beckoning us towards a little gate.

Stupid troll.

She's got no idea. I told her to keep out of sight and stay where she was, and here she is waving at us like a claphead. Anyone can see her from the house. There's nothing for it. We'll have to wig it to the gate before she does something even worse.

'Come on, Jaz. Run with me. Fast as you can.'

We haven't gone ten yards before there's a shout behind us.

'You!'

It's the old dunny. She's leaning out the lounge window pointing at us.

'Stop!'

Tammy's face appears, sees us, disappears. A moment later she's tearing round the side of the house towards us, followed by Sash and the other two trolls.

They're all carrying knives.

We'll never get away, not with Jaz slowing us down. The only chance is to get among people so the girls can't do too much. Becky's screaming for Jaz.

'Jaz, come here!'

I give the kid a push.

'Run to Fairypops!'

Jaz runs to the gate. Becky's already got it open. She calls out to me too.

'Come on!'

I'm waiting just a bit to give the trolls more to think about. They've already slowed, like they're not sure whether to go for me or Becky and the kid. Dunny's still peering out the window. They probably won't do much here, not with her watching.

I glance round. Jaz is through the gate and Becky's got her. I catch her eyes.

'Come on!' she says.

I run to the gate, push through, pull it closed.

Becky's picked up Jaz now. The kid's still clutching her picture. But here's Tammy and the others rushing the gate.

'Let's go!' says Becky.

She sets off down the path but she's running towards Hedley Woods.

'Becky! The other way! Into the city!'

We need people, not trees, but it's too late now. She's off down the path and the trolls are nearly on me. I turn and race after her but I'm choking, Bigeyes, I'm choking bad. We're in the grime and it's Becky's fault.

I should leave her to it but I know I can't, not with Jaz. I can't just blast off. But we're never going to handle four trolls. We can't fight 'em and we can't out-run 'em. Becky could outrun 'em on her own but not carrying Jaz. I've caught her up already.

And the trolls are close behind.

Here are the woods. They don't go far and if we stick to the path and run fast enough, we might meet some people on the way. But Becky's already branched off into the trees.

'Becky! Get back on the path!'

'No! We can lose 'em in the trees!'

'Get back on the path!'

She's not listening. She's running blind. We're blundering among oaks and beeches—and then suddenly she stops, turns, stares. It's like she's suddenly realized there's no point. She's still holding Jaz and they're both looking past me.

I stop too, turn and look.

They're coming towards us, all four, not hurrying now they've seen we've stopped. They're spreading out to cut off any escape. I stay where I am. No point in moving. I glance round.

Becky's moved back a few feet. She's put Jaz down and the two of them are standing by an old cedar. The little girl's still clutching her drawing. Doesn't look worried at all.

I wish I was her.

But I'm not. I'm me. Try as I might, I'm always me.

The trolls have stopped a few yards from me. I'm watching them but I can sense Becky and Jaz still standing behind me. I can sense the cedar tree even as I watch the faces before me.

Who's the worst now that Trixi's gone?

Hard to tell. Tammy and Sash are bad enough.

Can't remember the names of the other two. But I've seen 'em enough times. I know what they can do.

Becky calls out.

'Xen! Kat! You don't have to do what Tammy tells you!'

'Shut it!' says the black-haired girl.

'Xen—!'

'I said shut it!'

Becky tries the other girl.

'Kat, listen—'

'Don't even bother,' comes the answer.

And Becky falls silent.

So that's what they're called, Xen and Kat. But that's about as friendly as we're ever going to get. I'm watching Tammy. She's the nearest and she's clearly taken the lead. They're moving forward again. I give a shout.

'Stay back!'

'Shut your mouth, Slicky!' says Tammy.

'Stay back!'

'Going to stop us, are you?'

And that's when it happens.

That's the moment when I stop playing dead. One moment I'm a ghost, the next I'm standing there and the knife's out of my pocket and in my hand and the blade's open.

The girls stop, stare, glance at each other, back at me.

'Got a knife, Slicky?' says Sash. 'Know how to use it?'

'Becky didn't kill Trix,' I say. 'Neither did I.'

'Who did?'

Becky calls out behind me.

'Some guy. He was in the bungalow. I checked out one of the rooms while Trix checked out the main bedroom. I went in and found her lying dead. And this guy. He must have hit her over the head.'

I'm watching the trolls, one face at a time. They don't believe a word of this.

'It's true,' I say. 'I saw him.'

Tammy looks me up and down.

'You just happened to be there as well.'

'Yeah.'

She takes a step closer.

'So how come you're holding Trixi's knife?'

The other trolls stiffen. Tammy glances round at them.

'Didn't you notice?' she says to them. 'Slicky's got her knife.'

'I pulled it out of her pocket,' I say. 'To defend myself against the guy.'

'It's true,' says Becky.

But we're wasting our time. There's no point saying any more.

Sash is moving close too, and Xen, and Kat. Tammy snarls.

'You both had it in for Trix. Slicky cos of what we done on the towpath, and Bex cos Trixi told her she's yellow. But to take her out when she wasn't looking—'

'We didn't,' says Becky.

But it's too late for words now. They're coming forward. I hold up the knife, shout at them.

'Stay back!'

They come on. Behind me I feel Becky and Jaz moving by the tree.

'Stay back or—'

'Or what?' says Sash.

I glance over my shoulder. Becky and Jaz are still standing by the cedar, the little girl clutching her picture.

'Or what?' Sash says again.

And suddenly I'm shouting to the kid.

'Jaz, hold up your picture so we can see it! Hold it above your head!'

And without a word, without a murmur, she does what she always does. She does as she's told. She holds the picture above her head. Just an inch or two above. But it's enough.

Cos already my arm's whipping through the air. Only for me it's like slow motion. I'm seeing the past and the present and all time spinning as the knife flies through the air, the point racing towards the little girl standing by the tree. And I'm watching her face. It's just looking back, quiet and still, the quietest, stillest place in this whole stinking world.

The knife thuds into the picture and pins it to the tree.

The robin struck through the heart.

And I'm running over to Jaz. She's as still as before, as quiet and trusting as she ever was. Becky's screaming at me but I've got no time for her. I tug the knife free and the picture flutters to the ground. I turn and face the trolls. They haven't moved. They're staring. I feel Jaz take my free hand.

Becky falls silent.

I call out to the trolls.

'First person who comes forward gets the same.'

'Like Trixi got?' shouts Tammy.

'Not by me. Not by Becky.'

They go on staring, long, hard, then slowly turn and head off back through the woods. Becky touches me on the arm.

'It's not over,' she says.

I glance down at Jaz, her hand still in mine.

'It's just beginning,' I say.

It's not the best snug in the world, Bigeyes, but it'll do for tonight. And being a flat we can take a risk with the lights. Some of them anyway. Bedroom's OK, so's the lounge. There's dimmer switches in those rooms and the windows face out over the ring road. No one to see us but passing cars and we're too high up for anyone to care much about us.

Becky's been quiet all day. Hardly said a thing since we left the woods. Jaz doesn't say much either. Bit miffed that I messed up her picture but not for long. Keeps holding my hand.

Don't know where the rest of today's gone. Walking and watching, that's all I remember. And now it's eight in the evening, and it's dark, and my life's upside-down again.

It was good playing dead. I was sleeping my life out and it was sweet. I told you life's a whack. Trouble is, it's only a whack when you're in control. Rest of the time it's a dredge. I got to get a grip, got to sort out what to do. I've been a ghost for three years but now there's spectres after me again.

Becky's curled up on the sofa, Jaz with her. Little kid's sleeping, sleeping good. Becky's got her eyes closed too but she's not sleeping. She's trying to block me out, block everything out. She's trying to forget.

Don't ask me how I know.

Only it won't work. Cos you don't forget. You don't ever forget. The spectres come back wherever you go.

Can't make this troll out. She's not like Tammy and the rest. They're hard but she's beaten up, or beaten down, or both. She's certainly a dimpy mother. There's no way I'd leave a kid like Jaz with a crazy old dunny whose lights have gone out and who let duffs off the street use her house for a drug den.

I wouldn't let Jaz out of my sight for two minutes if she was my kid.

But I'll tell you one thing about Becky—Trixi was wrong about her. The girl's not yellow. She's just scared and that's not the same thing at all. She's still got her eyes closed, see? But I'm telling you, she's wide awake, and she's thinking hard.

Like I am.

Feels strange showing one of my snugs to someone. Haven't told her much about it. Guy who owns it works on an oil rig. One month on, one month off. I found out about him a couple of years ago and I've been keeping a check on where he is ever since. He won't be back here for another three weeks.

Got a lot going for it, this place. Old-fashioned lock, easy to pick. Ancient gobbo next door with a hearing problem. Empty flat on the other side. Only reason I don't come here more often is cos there's no books to read.

Becky's opened her eyes.

'You all right, Bex?'

She answers with a question.

'Where'd you learn to throw a knife like that?'

I was wondering when she'd bring this up. She's been carefully avoiding it all day.

'Doesn't matter where I learned it.'

'Is that your way of telling me to mind my own business?'

'Maybe.'

Silence. She's watching me hard now. Her eyes are blacker than ever with the lights on so low. She looks down at Jaz, still sleeping beside her, then back at me.

'Do that to my kid again and I'll kill you.'

'I might just have saved her life. And yours.'

'You could have killed her.'

'But I didn't. And here we are. I've done everything I promised. I've found you a doss. I've given you some food.'

'You call that food? Can of beans, can of mush, can of sweetcorn?'

'I can't help it if the guy's got nothing else in the flat. He usually has some soup here.'

She looks away. She's fizzing with pain, fizzing with anger. She pulls out a cig.

'Don't,' I say.

She looks at me.

'No cigs, Bex.'

'What the hell does it matter?'

'I don't leave traces in the snugs I use.'

She stares at me, more angry than ever. I'm probably being stupid. Open the window and the smoke'll be gone by the time he gets back. But I'm so used to leaving nothing behind.

Maybe it doesn't matter. Maybe I'll just give up this snug, not use it any more. Cos I'm starting to think something, Bigeyes. I'm starting to think this city's done for. They're here now. The spectres are back. No place'll be safe any more. All that I've built up here, all that I've learned from my hours of watching, counts for nothing.

I've got to start again.

Somewhere else.

Maybe they'll find me there too. But I've got to start again. And somehow I've got to hope.

Becky speaks again.

'I'll keep my promise.'

I look at her.

'I'll be gone in the morning,' she says. 'Out of your life.'

There's a long silence. Outside the flat I can hear cars pounding along the ring road. They're like distant voices, people I don't know going to places I don't know, speaking to no one.

My life's so dark now.

What happened to the light?

Remember that book I showed you last night? About a guy called Nietzsche? *Superman and the Will to Power.* There's something he says in it.

What doesn't destroy me makes me stronger.

Do you believe that, Bigeyes?

I don't know. I look at Becky and I don't know. I look at myself and I don't know. I look at you and I don't know. I don't even know if you're listening.

I don't feel stronger. I feel weak and small. I'm still here but I feel weak and small.

'Is that what you want?' says Becky.

I look back at her. She looks weak and small too.

The only one here who looks strong is Jaz, lying there fast asleep.

'Is that what you want?' says Becky again. 'Me and Jaz to go?'

I look at her. I look at Jaz. I hear myself speak.

'No.'

Dawn. Gutter-grey. Rumble of cars still there. Haven't slept much. I turn on the radio. Been avoiding it but I got to know the worst.

'The news headlines. Police are hunting a girl of sixteen, named as Rebecca Jakes, and a boy of around fourteen, going by the nickname Slicky, in connection with the murder of a sixteen-year-old girl in the Carnside district of the city. The victim, whose name has not yet been made public, was found bludgeoned to death in a small—'

Becky switches it off.

'Don't want to hear that,' she says.

'We need to know what they know.'

'We already know what they know.'

She looks over at Jaz. She's sitting in the corner,

drawing another picture on the back of the one I messed up, ignoring the hole in the middle where the knife went through.

'Bex, we need to know what they're saying on the news.'

She looks back at me, lowers her voice.

'The police were looking for me before I came here. But I met Trixi and the gang and went to ground at Tammy's gran's. I been keeping out of sight since then. But they'll know I'm here now. As for you . . .'

She runs her eye over me.

'You're a story in yourself.'

'We need some breakfast.'

'Don't change the subject.'

'We still need some breakfast.'

'Who are those men looking for you?'

'Never seen 'em before.'

'But they know who you are. That man called you Blade. And he was right about that, wasn't he? You can't kid anyone about that now.'

I give a shrug. But it doesn't shake her off that easily.

'So who are they?' she says.

'Just guys sent by other people.'

'What other people?'

'I've made a few enemies.'

'Like who?'

'Like it's time for breakfast.'

I stand up, walk over to Jaz.

'Hey, Jaz!'

She looks up.

'What are you drawing?'

She shows me the picture. Another bird.

'That's nice,' I say. 'I promise not to mess it up this time. You hungry?'

She nods.

'I'll see what we got.'

And there won't be much. The guy stocks up with cans of this and that but not much else. I head for the kitchen. Becky joins me and we hunt through the cupboards.

'There's some porridge oats,' she says. 'We could make that with some water. What else is there?'

'Some crispbread.' I'm hunting through another cupboard. 'Bit of marmalade. Any margarine?'

She pulls open the fridge.

'Yeah.' Takes the top off and sniffs it. 'Seems OK.'

We eat breakfast, wash up, stack away. Weird silence hanging over us. Guy next door's got his television on loud. Clatter at the door and a bundle of letters drops through to join the heap on the floor. Jaz goes back to her drawing. Becky and me sit at the table.

'We got to get away, Bex.'

'I know,' she says. 'When?'

'Tonight. When it's good and dark.'

'What we going to do today?'

'Stay here. Stay out of sight.'

'The owner won't come back?'

'Not unless he's a good swimmer.'

Silence. I look at her. She's like a little girl again, like Jaz almost. Only Jaz isn't scared.

'I'm scared too, Bex.'

'I thought it was just me.'

I shake my head.

And it's true, Bigeyes. I'm choked out. Cos I know it's all over. Everything's changed. I was free before. I was on top of my mountain, remember? And now the police want me, the gang want me, and what's worse—the past wants me too. It's reaching out again like a corpse waking up.

Like it is for Becky.

'I'm scared too, Bex.'

She looks at me.

'Where are we going to go?'

'Away.'

'Can't we hide in the city?'

'No.'

'But you must know it really well.'

'I know it better than anybody. That's why I know we've got to go. There are too many people looking for us round here.'

'So where can we go?'

'Don't know. Get away first and then decide.'

She looks over her shoulder at Jaz. The little girl's frowning over her picture, like nothing else matters.

'Bex?'

She looks back at me.

'You got any money?' I say.

'No. You?'

'No. What about other stuff?'

'Couple of things back at Tammy's gran's house. Nothing I can't leave.'

'OK.'

'We got to wait, then? Till tonight?'

'Yeah.'

So we wait. Jaz draws, covers the paper, asks for more. Becky finds a pad of lined paper and another pencil and the two of them draw together. As for me, I think.

About all the things I've tried to forget—and for a moment it's like I'm seven years old again. I want to stand in the road like I used to and stop the traffic, and shout and swear and tell the whole world to go to hell. Only now it's all different. Cos this time they won't just watch. This time they'll run me down.

It's like my whole life's unravelled. I had it all tight like a little ball, but it was a ball of wool, and now someone's chucked it and the thing's rolling away, leaving the thread behind for all to follow.

Didn't take much to find me after all.

The gobbos and that hairy grunt must have been tracking me for ages, must have seen me with the trolls on the towpath, or maybe just afterwards heading for the bungalow. They certainly knew I was in there. It was me they were coming for when they smashed their way in.

And now Trixi's dead and probably Mary too.

How many more people are going to get rubbed out cos of me?

I'm looking at Becky, looking at Jaz, and I'm feeling choked again.

Day moves on like a slow dream.

And then evening comes.

We eat again, same meal as before. No one's speaking. It's like we're waiting for an execution. Television's still loud next door. Been on all day but I've hardly noticed it. We wash up, clear away, sit down again. Becky looks pale.

'Bex?'

'What?'

'Do you want to ring the police?'

'You kidding?'

'I don't mean to give yourself up. I mean to tell 'em about the guy who killed Trixi. And the other two who turned up. It'll give the police other people to look out for. Might even help you.'

She shakes her head.

'I'm in enough trouble with the police as it is. There's no way they're going to believe anything I say. Anyway . . . '

She doesn't need to finish. I already know she's scared of the porkers.

I stand up.

'Come on, then. We got to go.'

Becky stands up and holds out her hand to Jaz. The little girl takes it but looks up at me.

'You ready, Jaz?' I say.

She nods.

And then I remember something.

'Bex?'

'Yeah?'

'Take this, can you?'

I hold out the knife.

'I don't want it,' she says.

'Neither do I.'

'But you're the one who knows how to use it.'

I know it too well, Bigeyes. That's the problem. I know the knife too well. Like I know the city too well. It's time to leave both behind.

'Take it, Bex. Please.'

She takes it, puts it in her pocket.

'Thanks,' I say.

I look round, check the flat, turn off the lights, open the door. All still. Corridor's dark and silent. Even next door's gone quiet.

We step out, wait, listen. Nothing moves, nothing murmurs. Just the sound of the traffic outside. Becky closes the door. Listen again, then down the stairs, soft and slow, floor by floor, and finally out and off into the night.

tim bowler

CLOSING IN

In the next instalment of Blade . . .

There's enough people looking for us.
The police, the girl gang, all the others.
I don't like to think about it. But the past
has come back, hooked its claws into me.
LIFE's DANGEROUS AGAIN . . .

I reach into my pocket, squeeze the knife, hold it tight.
'Keep it,' she says.
I let go, pull my hand out. The knife feels heavy in my pocket, heavier than it should. I don't know why.
'I'll see you,' I say.
And I'm gone.

Piece of cake getting in. They got a burglar alarm but they only had sensors put in the hall, front room and main bedroom. I suppose they think that's all they need. They've obviously got their valuables in those rooms. But I'm not after their valuables.
There's other stuff I want more . . .

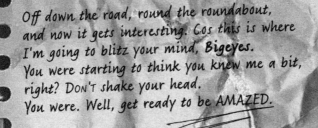

Off down the road, round the roundabout, and now it gets interesting. Cos this is where I'm going to blitz your mind, **Bigeyes**.
You were starting to think you knew me a bit, right? DON'T shake your head.
You were. Well, get ready to be AMAZED.

Tim Bowler is one of the UK's most compelling and original writers for teenagers. He was born in Leigh-on-Sea in Essex and after studying Swedish at university, he worked in forestry, the timber trade, teaching and translating before becoming a full-time writer. He lives with his wife in a small village in Devon and his work-room is an old stone outhouse known to friends as 'Tim's Bolthole'.

Tim has written eight novels and won twelve awards, including the prestigious Carnegie Medal for *River Boy*. His most recent novel is the electrifying *Frozen Fire* and his provocative new *BLADE* series is already being hailed as a groundbreaking work of fiction. He has been described by the *Sunday Telegraph* as 'the master of the psychological thriller' and by the *Independent* as 'one of the truly individual voices in British teenage fiction'.